Serpent

Nicholas Mosley was born in 1923. He is the author of twelve novels, including *Accident*, *Impossible Object* and the other four volumes of the *Catastrophe Practice* series, *Catastrophe Practice*, *Imago Bird*, *Judith* and *Hopeful Monsters*. He has also written two biographies, a travel book and a book about religion. Nicholas Mosley is married, has five children, and lives in London.

This edition of *Serpent* has a text substantially revised from that of the original Secker & Warburg edition (1981).

NICHOLAS MOSLEY
Serpent

Minerva

A Minerva Paperback
SERPENT

First published in Great Britain 1981
by Martin Secker & Warburg Limited
This revised Minerva edition published 1991
by Mandarin Paperbacks
Michelin House, 81 Fulham Road, London SW3 6RB

Minerva is an imprint of the Octopus Publishing Group,
a division of Reed International Books Limited

A CIP catalogue record for this title
is available from the British Library
ISBN 0 7493 9922 8

Printed and bound in Great Britain
by Cox and Wyman Ltd, Reading, Berks.

Serpent

I

As Jason stepped into the body of the aeroplane he thought —
What does this remind me of? this hollow containing people
staring at a blank wall: some image of the mind that for thousands of years has been in the mind: Plato's cave, where people
sit with their backs to the sun and see the shadows cast on the
wall in front; their intimations of reality. And they do not turn
to the sun. He hit his head, gently, on the top of the doorway
into the plane. An air hostess put out a hand too late to stop
him. He smiled at her; he thought — Perhaps we stay facing the
wall because the shadows are manipulated by such vestal
virgins. He turned towards the first-class compartment at the
front of the plane. Here the seats were widely spaced and half
empty; behind, in the tourist compartment, the seats were
tightly packed and crowded. He thought — This is an image of
the conscious and the unconscious?

The hostess said 'First-class?'

He said 'Yes.'

He found he wanted to say — I'm afraid so.

The hostess said 'We thought we'd lost you.'

In the first-class compartment there were three rows of
seats each with two seats on either side of the aisle. The two at
the front on the right were occupied, as were the two on the
right at the back. On the left there was just one very large man
in the middle row by the window. Jason thought — The others
are keeping as far away from him as they can: he is like God to
them —

Then — But if this is an image of the left and the right sides of
the brain, is it not the left that represents rationality and the
right divinity?

He stopped by the empty seat next to the large man by the
window. The man wore a cloak which hung over the arm of the

empty seat so that he was like a drop of oil, and spreading.

Jason said 'Shall I sit here?'

The large man said 'If you must.'

When he turned to Jason there was his huge expressionless face like a globe with just reflections of rainbows on it.

Jason put down his bag on the floor. The man made no move to withdraw his cloak.

He said 'We thought we'd lost you.'

Jason said 'I got caught up.'

The large man said 'By the apron strings?'

The door by which Jason had entered the plane was being closed. There was the voice of an air hostess over the loud-speakers telling the passengers to fasten their seat-belts and to keep their seats in an upright position.

Jason said 'I've got to talk to you.'

The large man said 'What's stopping you.'

Jason sat down. He thought — You will cast your thunder-bolts for a time; then you will suddenly be charming.

He said 'About my script.'

The large man said 'What do you want to talk about the script?'

Jason stared ahead towards the captain's cabin. He thought — In this symbolic world, in which we are trapped like patterns of thinking within brain cells —

— Those two people on the right at the front, the two on the right at the back, Epstien and myself on the left in the middle —

He said 'I don't think you'll like what I've written. It's come out differently from what we talked about. I mean, I think it had to come out different.'

The large man beside him, who was a film producer called Epstien, said 'You tell me this now?'

The plane was trundling over the ground, bumping and rolling lethargically.

Jason said 'Now I can tell you.'

He thought — You will understand that I mean you will be trapped for the next four hours.

Epstien said 'You mean, if you go on telling me I won't like what you've written, I may like it?'

2

Jason laughed. He thought — I must remember he is clever.

He said 'I don't think you'll make the film.'

Epstien said 'Why not?'

Jason said 'It'll break taboos.'

He thought — But he may not want to be thought someone who does not want to break taboos?

Then — But still, I am doing this too quickly: I should be making charming noises at him; explaining why I nearly missed the plane; checking up what these other people with him are doing, to make him feel somewhat godlike —

— But I do not want him to make this film?

Epstien said 'What taboos?'

Jason said 'Against one talking about life being a successfully going concern. About the probable cost of this.'

Epstien was sitting back with his eyes closed. He was holding on to the sides of his seat.

Jason thought — It was God who gave men the gift of language to confuse them, when he thought they were being too successful building a tower to heaven?

Then Epstien said 'How is she?'

'Who?'

'The apron strings.'

Jason thought — Well, yes: this is, is it not, a move to confuse me.

When he had been in the departure lounge of the airport it was true that he, Jason, had been having a row with his wife, Lilia. Lilia had been booked to travel on the same aeroplane as he, but in the tourist-class. She had said 'I don't mind your being first-class and me tourist if it's only you the film people will pay for, but I don't see why I can't come up and talk to you.' He had said 'I'd have paid for you to be first-class, but I've got to talk to them.' She had said 'Well I won't stop you.' He had thought — Yes you will. He had said 'But if you come up, Epstien will stop me.'

Now, in the first-class compartment, he said 'She's very well, thank you.'

Epstien said 'I hear you've married her.'

Jason said 'This is another one.'

Epstien said 'Dear God, there are two?'

Jason thought — Well, that's quite witty.

In the departure lounge he had tried to explain to Lilia — 'You see, Epstien's difficult with women: he's difficult with everyone, he thinks he has to dominate them, to blow hot and cold: but with women he's like a wind tunnel.' Lilia had said 'But won't that actress be with you?' Jason had said 'Yes that actress will be with us.' Lilia had said 'You don't want me to come up because that actress will be with you.'

In the first-class compartment Epstien said 'I've heard of her. I haven't met her?'

Jason said 'No.'

Epstien was breathing heavily. The aeroplane was turning on to a runway.

Jason thought — In Plato's cave people did not talk? It was like a cinema?

In the departure lounge he had tried to explain to Lilia — 'But you don't know these film people, they're prima donnas, they're obsessed with power. They talk of artistry, or truth, or love, or whatever; but like this they can get more power. If you want to have anything to do with film people, you've got to know you're dealing with power.'

Lilia had said 'Then why are you a film person?'

He had said 'Well I soon won't be.'

She had said 'I suppose you mean because of me.'

He had said 'No I mean because of what I've written.'

She had said 'Then why did you write it?'

He had said 'I suppose because I want to stop being a film person.'

He had thought — That's quite clever.

She had said 'Then why do you mind if I come up and talk to you and Epstien?'

He had thought — Well, that's clever too.

Then — I have to go out fighting!

Now, in the first-class compartment, he wondered if he should say to Epstien — You see, my wife is in the tourist-class —

— But then Epstien might say — Why doesn't she come up here?

4

— And she might not even have got on the plane!

But he was sure she had.

The last time he had worked with Epstien, in Rome, he had been with the girl he had lived with before he had met Lilia. Epstien had been hostile to her. He had said — You pick women to torment you and to interfere with your work. Jason had said — Perhaps those are the conditions under which I can work. Epstien had said — Well are they or aren't they? He had said — Well, we'll see. But even then he had thought — That's not the point: we are what we make of ourselves: we are out of the Garden of Eden.

Now the aeroplane was taking off into a bright sky.

Jason, sitting beside Epstien, thought — You warned me —

Then — But was not God jealous of humans when they got out of the Garden of Eden?

He said 'What I want to talk about — '

Epstien remained with his eyes closed.

Jason thought — He is frightened of flying?

Then — God sulks, because he is still trapped in Eden?

When Jason had been having his row with Lilia in the departure lounge their child, who was to travel with Lilia in the tourist-class, had watched them with dark, troubled eyes. He had from time to time tried to put his head between Lilia and Jason. Jason had thought — His eyes are like sailing boats scudding before a storm. Lilia had said 'It's just that you always put your work before me.' Jason had said 'But I'm taking you to a holiday by the Red Sea.' Lilia had said 'But only after your work.' Jason had said 'What do you expect me to do about my work?' Lilia had said 'What do you expect me to do in the meantime?' Jason had wanted to say — Oh go home! Lilia had said 'Do you want me to go home?'

Their child, who was aged four, had put his hands against her face as if he were a sculptor choosing marble from a mountain.

Jason thought — It is a child that God, or Epstien, would be jealous of?

The aeroplane was moving up through the bright sky.

Epstien said 'What is it you want to talk to me about?'

Jason said 'It's not really that I think that a film of such a subject can't be made. I just think it would be very difficult.'

Epstien said 'You want it to be made.'

Jason thought — Do I?

Epstien said 'What are these taboos that will stop it?'

Jason said 'About life being a successfully going concern. Nearly all films, nearly all stories, are either tragedy or farce.'

Epstien said 'Or cynical — '

'Or cynical.'

'Or sentimental — '

Jason said ' — And so not true.'

Epstien said 'What happened between you and her in the airport lounge?'

Jason thought — He will go to and fro like lights switched on and off in an interrogation room.

He said 'The reason why stories are tragic or farcical or cynical or sentimental is that they would make people uncomfortable if they were not — if they were true.'

Then — 'My wife Lilia wanted to come up here into the first-class. But I told her I had to talk to you.'

He thought — But it's true, is it not, that these contexts are similar?

Epstien said 'She's on the plane?'

Jason said 'Yes.'

Epstien said 'Then why doesn't she come up here?'

Jason thought — It's by seeing two things at once, that one might see whether or not they are true?

He said 'The thing is, if one showed a film about life being a successfully going concern, people would think you were getting at them, and would walk out of the cinema.'

Epstien said 'She walked out of the airport lounge?'

Jason said 'No, I did.'

Epstien said 'And then what did you do?

'I came to look for you.'

'Where?'

'In the VIP lounge.'

'But we were in the VIP lounge.'

'I know. I couldn't face seeing you.'

Jason thought — I imagine I can impress Epstien, or myself, by saying what is true?

Epstien said 'And what was that, tragedy or farce?'

'Neither.'

'Why not?'

'Well here I am.'

'And where's your wife?'

'On the plane.'

'How do you know?'

'Well that's the point; I just do.'

Jason thought — And even if she isn't, would it make any difference to what I believe is true?

Epstien sat with his hands on his knees staring at the blank wall in front.

Jason thought — I can explain: You see, why else were Lilia and I having this row? except to show that she was upset at not being with me —

Epstien said 'You think people would be envious, if they saw a film about life being a successfully going concern?'

Jason thought — Yes.

He bent down to a bag on the floor at his feet. He said 'See what I've written.'

He pulled a typescript out of the bag. He held it on his knee. He turned over some pages.

He said 'I've written a short piece on why the film can't be made. This, as you've seen, might help to get something made. Then I've sketched out a few scenes of the sort of thing that might conceivably, if one wants to do something interesting, be done.'

He held out the script to Epstien. He thought — I'm mad to be doing this?

Epstien sat with his hands on his knees. He said 'But why do you think that you and your wife are not to do with tragedy or farce?'

Jason said 'How else could she have shown that she minded?'

'Minded what?'

'That she wasn't with me.'

'Or what you've written?'

Jason thought — Yes, that's true.

He sat holding the script out to Epstien.

Epstien said 'And why is your script not tragedy or farce?'

Jason said 'Because it's to do with how tragedy or farce might be used.'

'And that is taboo?'

'To talk about it. Yes.'

'Why?'

Jason sat holding out the script.

After a time Epstien took it. He held it on his knee. He read — *The reason why it is unlikely that this film should be made is that it would be morally and politically objectionable.*

He said 'And you think you've found a way of talking that is not.'

Jason said 'Perhaps only because it wouldn't be much understood.'

Epstien said 'Then what's the point of that?'

'People will make what they want of it.'

'Those who want to will think it tragedy or farce — '

'And those who won't — '

Jason thought — But if he's so clever, why doesn't he make better films?

Epstien said ' — And those who won't, will know things like that your wife's on the plane.'

Jason thought — Dear God, if he's so clever, might he actually make this film?

Epstien sat holding the typescript on his knee. Jason thought — He is like one of those statues staring out over the banks of the Nile —

Epstien said 'Why don't you write a script about you and your women?'

Jason said 'Perhaps I have.'

Epstien said 'What happened to the last?'

Jason said 'She's all right.'

He thought — Is it just God the Father's size, that makes one think he should not be jealous?

Epstien said 'Do you think in fact I'll make this film?'

Jason said 'No I don't.'

Epstien said 'Why not?'

Jason thought — Because you'll think you'll want to survive?

Then — Or rather, because you won't be interested in looking at how anyone might survive?

He said 'There should be some way of doing it.'

Epstien said 'You have to think that people are all right?'

II

Lilia had watched Jason go off in the departure lounge of the airport and had thought — Well, he won't go far: he'll hide for a time, in the lavatory or somewhere, and then he'll go to the VIP lounge to find his smart friends. He'll know, surely, that this row is because I mind I can't sit next to him on the plane; and he should be glad, because this shows I love him, doesn't it, O Jason. She was holding in her arms her child who was trying to pull at her face as if it were plasticine. She said 'Oh do shut up!' She thought — Life consists of things like wanting to sit next to each other on planes and knowing one should not: and so one has rows, to demonstrate that everything is all right. But you do know this, don't you, O Jason.

She said to her child 'Daddy's going to be on the plane!' The child said 'Then why is Daddy gone away?' She wanted to say — Daddy's silly. She said 'Daddy's sad he's not going to sit next to us on the plane.' Her child said 'Daddy's silly.' She said 'Daddy's not silly.' She wondered if she could explain — You see, it's just part of us that wants to make out Daddy's silly, so we won't be so sad he can't sit next to us on the plane.

When the time came for her to move from the departure lounge to the room where passengers assembled before getting onto the plane she found herself tearful: she thought — There is all this cleverness! but still, I may be picked up by a violent man or someone and then something may happen such as what happens in books that one buys in airports about planes: I will be seduced, or held hostage, or blown up, or something. I know it is reasonable for you to travel first-class and for us to travel tourist, O Jason, but when have people ever been reasonable? In the room where passengers assembled there were further security checks: luggage and hand-luggage had already been searched: now there was a metal-detector machine and an X-ray machine and a body-search. She thought — And Jason will be sweeping through unmolested with all his smart friends! unless, that is, those old queens, like flies, enjoy having hands up their legs. Lilia was carrying a zip-bag, a handbag, a push-chair, and her child. She thought — My God, I have forgotten to get whisky! It is your fault, O Jason: I bet you haven't forgotten whisky!

The second set of security precautions, she imagined, was to do with their going to Israel. Passengers were queuing up in front of the metal-detector machine as if it were a revolving door. Lilia thought — I expect at this stage you would make one of your witty remarks, O Jason, such as its being as difficult to get through the eye of a metal-detector machine as into the kingdom of Israel. There was a man at the head of the queue whom she had noticed before in the departure lounge: he was a dark-skinned, curly-haired young man who might be an Arab or a Jew: he wore a fur-lined anorak and tight jeans: he looked exactly the sort of man who might be going to blow up a plane — or do that other thing, she joked to herself, that men are supposed to do to girls who are alone on planes. She had put down her child and he had run to the head of the queue and was now by the man staring up at the bar at the top of the metal-detector machine. Lilia thought — But if that man looks exactly like the sort of man who would be going to blow up a plane, wouldn't it be unlikely if he was? but then, if he really was going to blow up a plane, wouldn't he perhaps want to look exactly like a man going to blow up a plane so that people would think this unlikely — this, or the other thing? Her child, by the metal-detector machine, stretched up his arms. The man, standing by him, suddenly bent down, picked him up, and held him aloft, as if he might swing from the crossbar. The child looked down at the man. Lilia thought — Like a cherub from a ceiling. Then — They are an extraordinarily handsome couple.

The man stepped forward, put the child down, squatted, and seemed to be talking to the child.

Lilia thought — But he has not been through the metal-detector machine —

— He has used the child to get past without going through the metal-detector machine.

The officials did not seem to be paying any attention to the man; as if events were not serious, when people were playing with children.

Lilia wondered if she should say — But he and the child have not been through the metal-detector machine!

— To get us into the kingdom of heaven?

When it came to her turn to go through her child was still with the man, slightly past the machine. The man was chatting with one of the girls who were officials. Lilia thought — Perhaps he is himself a security guard: and so he would not have to go through a metal-detector machine. But then, why pick up the child?

— In order to pick up me?

— In those trousers, which are so tight they could hardly be carrying a gun or something —

— Unless it is so exactly the same shape as his something-or-other —

She said to her child 'Have you been through?'

The girl by the machine said 'Yes.'

Lilia thought — Well, one cannot organise the kingdom of heaven.

She had to collect from the X-ray machine her handbag, her camera, her zip-bag, and the push-chair. She thought — But if the man is trying to pick me up, do I or do I not let him know I know this? Or first, do I or do I not want this?

The man was at her side, picking up her child again and handing him to her.

She said 'Thank you.'

She began piling her luggage into the push-chair.

She thought — If I appear not to be able to look at him, this will or will not make him think that I think he is trying to pick me up —

— So it seems I do want him to do this?

Then — Is not all this too corny: just because you are with your smart friends, O Jason!

While they were waiting by the doorway before boarding

the plane the man went and sat on a chair to one side of the queue and he put his head in his hands. Lilia thought — He is ill: or he wants me to think he is ill, so it will be easier for him to pick me up?

Her child said 'Mummy — '

She said 'Yes?'

Her child said 'That man's got sweeties in his bag!'

She thought she might say — Well, that's one way of putting it.

She said 'What else did he say?'

Her child laughed.

She thought — Those knowing eyes: what is it that children have remembered?

When the time came for her to go on to the plane — she had been allowed to go to the head of the queue because of her child — the man was still sitting with his head in his hands. She thought — Well, it's just as well he wasn't trying to pick me up; now I can go on being outraged by Jason and those old queens in the first-class. She walked carrying her child and her bags on to the plane; there was a curtain drawn between the area where she went in, by the steward's cabin, and the first-class. She wondered — Are they already on the plane? shall I stick my head through the curtain and make a face like Punch or Judy? Then — Why does one want to be outraged by things like old queens in the first-class? A hostess had taken her push-chair: she turned right and moved towards the back of the plane. She thought — I don't want to be too close to the first-class because then Jason might see me and might not be worried that we might not be on the plane; but I don't want to be too far back, because then I'll be one of the last to get a drink and food which usually come from the direction of the first-class. She decided on a row about eight rows back; she put down her child on the seat nearest to the window. She thought — But what if Jason, because of our quarrel, is not on the plane? Then — But you would not have done anything so outrageous as that, O Jason?

When she had settled next to her child in the middle seat of three and was checking through her zip-bag for biscuits, orange juice, picture book, fire-engine —

— And was thinking: What makes us want to play games like wanting or not wanting to be picked up by men on planes? or to be outraged by people in the first-class? or even to appear to have missed the plane? Is it, as you so often say, O Jason, simply that by this sort of thing, this battling, people know where they are —

— But do you not also say that it is nice both to know where one is, and not: to be one's own cake, and to eat it —

— Like St Lawrence on his grid-iron —

— Whatever that means.

When she was feeling rather sad that she had not responded more actively to the man with curly hair and tight jeans —

There was someone in the aisle waiting to move into the seat beside her.

She said 'Sorry!' and moved out of the way her handbag and her child's favourite toy, the fire-engine.

Then she realised the person in the aisle was the curly-haired man with tight jeans.

She thought — So he has been trying to pick me up all the time!

She was pleased. Then she thought — Dear God, as Jason would say, watch out when you are pleased!

The man was settling down beside her in the seat by the aisle. He was putting some luggage on the floor in front of him.

She thought — But in the room where we assembled, he did not have any luggage!

Then — This is what people do, isn't it, who want to blow up planes? They get an accomplice to leave a bag somewhere past the security checks with bombs and guns and things; and then when they have been through the metal-detector machine —

— But he has not been through the metal-detector machine —

— So does this or does this not mean —

— I am thinking all this to distract me?

She said to the child 'There!' and gave him a picture book, a biscuit, and the fire-engine.

She thought — Where's the fire, brother —

— In your great big beautiful eyes?

Then — The reason why people think about people blowing up planes is to distract them from thoughts of the same sort of people in tight jeans?

Her child said 'Mummy — '

She said 'Yes?'

Her child said 'That man's got sweeties — '

She said 'That man has not got sweeties!'

The man was bending over his bag on the floor. Poking out of it, there was what seemed to be the top of a bottle of whisky.

Lilia thought she might turn to the man and say — All right, please, may I have some of the sweeties in your bag?

Then the man leaned back and closed his eyes and held his stomach as if he were in pain.

Lilia thought — Or he is praying?

— For guidance? for forgiveness? for being about to blow up the plane?

— There was that film, was there not, about a man who wanted to get life-insurance for his wife —

Then — Oh why did you leave me in this terrible predicament, O Jason!

The man screwed up his face and rocked backwards and forwards.

Then Lilia thought — He is an actor?

— Now why did I think that?

Jason sometimes said — You can tell what is acting and what is not, but you can't tell how you can tell —

— Actors are people who know that they are acting.

The people in the tourist-class had settled down in their seats. The hostess by the doorway seemed to be waiting for some late arrival to come on the plane.

Lilia tried to go back in her mind to exactly what had happened between Jason and herself in the departure lounge. She did not really know why she and Jason had these rows. She had just wanted to make sure that, as soon as he had finished his work on this so-called reconnaissance trip for the film, he would join her and the child in their hotel by the sea. Jason had thought she was trying to interfere with his work. But of course, all this was nonsense. All rationalisations were

15

nonsense. Even hers. So what was happening?

The man beside her had turned his face towards her. He had small, neat features and precisely cut hair. He was, it was true, like a minor film star. He seemed to be about to speak: then he turned away and clenched his teeth.

She remembered Jason saying — The thing you know about actors is, that they are people who know their messages are false.

She wondered — But you meant, that is correct, because all our messages are false?

Then — What was the name of that film about the man and his insurance —

Then — Or perhaps it is just that this man's sweeties have got caught in the zip of his bags?

— Ha ha.

She wondered if she should say — Can I help you?

Her child said 'Mummy — '

She said 'Yes?'

Her child said 'That man — '

She said 'If you say that once more I'll scream.'

The man was now peering round towards the first-class. She thought — But he really is rather beautiful.

Her child said 'Where's Daddy?'

She said 'In the first-class.'

She thought — Was that a false move, to let the man know I've got a husband in the first-class?

— False with regard to what?

Then — He might know my messages are false?

Her child said 'What's the first-class?'

She said 'Where they have champagne and caviare and things.'

She could never quite remember how her quarrels with Jason escalated. One minute they were having a perfectly reasonable discussion, and the next minute he was walking off as if he had insulted her. She thought — I mean, as if I had insulted him. He had said — You don't know these film people, they are prima donnas. She had said — You think, being married to you, I don't know about prima donnas? She had only wanted to point out, that since the film might now not be made, he might be able to join her earlier by the Red Sea. She thought — Oh I know I am doing this rationalising only to cover up! But he'd begun to lecture her in his quiet, reasonable way —

— Just because I'm going to say that the film probably can't be made, doesn't mean I don't have to say what I have to say about it —

— and so on —

— So what was he trying to cover up?

The dark man beside her had picked up his bag and was holding it tightly to his middle.

She thought — Ah, I know! He's a junkie in need of a fix!

Then — Do I mean, that makes it all right?

She tried to remember another image Jason was always going on about — how people were like things sitting and seeing only shadows on the back wall of a cave —

— But why, Jason would say, did they not turn to the sun outside?

She had never seen the point of that question. She had always thought — Well it just wouldn't have struck them to, would it?

The curtain had been drawn at the front of the tourist-class. The door seemed to be being shut beyond it at the entrance to the plane. The voice of an air hostess was telling passengers to fasten their seat-belts, and to ensure that their seats were in an upright position.

Her child said 'I want a drink.'

She said 'So do we all, darling.'

Bending down to get at the child's orange juice and wondering whether, if she encouraged the man, he would offer her some whisky —

— She noticed his shoes, which were of very expensive soft leather.

She thought — Dear God, some smell, as of a hot hotel room, in a desert —

Then — Where did that image come from?

Then — Images are quite at random, aren't they?

When she straightened she saw that the man was delving into the bag at his middle —

— For his bomb? his gun? his fix?

If Jason had been with her she would have whispered —

— What shall we do? —

— About what? —

— Him —

— And Jason would have pretended not to know what she was talking about for a time; and then would have put his hand on his heart and rolled his eyes like St Sebastian —

Her child said 'Mummy — '

She said 'Yes?'

Her child said 'Will you ask that man — '

She said 'No I will not ask that man!'

She thought — Well, after all, I might get some whisky.

She handed orange juice to the child.

She thought — And Jason will be flirting with those film stars —

— And all is for the best in the best of all possible worlds —

— Isn't that what you say, O Jason?

She said to the man beside her 'Excuse me, could you possibly tell my child that you have not got sweeties in that bag?'

The man said nothing.

She said ' — Or he'll go on for the rest of the journey.'

The man still seemed to be in pain, or praying.

Lilia thought — Well, I've done my best: to have my cake, to know where I am, and eat it.

Then — Perhaps he doesn't speak English.

At least she could now look at him more closely. There was a slight scar on the brown cheek closest to her. His mouth seemed dusty. His skin was like his shoes: soft, to be trodden on by —

She thought — Dear God, I need that whisky!

The plane was trundling on to a runway.

She thought — What is that other thing Jason goes on about — how what's interesting is not what happens, but the connections —

She bent down to her zip-bag again and rummaged in it. She

brought out a copy of Jason's typescript.

Then the man beside her seemed to say in a quiet, desperate voice — 'I have got sweeties.'

She heard herself say 'What?'

She thought — I didn't hear correctly?

The man was still clutching his middle.

She thought — He has eaten something that has poisoned him?

She was looking at the first page of Jason's typescript. She read — *The reason why it is unlikely that this film should be made* —

The man said 'Can you help me?'

III

Epstien, in the first-class compartment of the aeroplane, held the first four pages of Jason's typescript and read —

The reason why it is unlikely that this film should be made is that it would be morally and politically objectionable. By morally, I mean according to what has become acceptable by custom.

The story, as those who have read my original suggestions for a screenplay will know, is to do with the war between the Jews and the Romans from 66 to 73 A.D. The Jews were trying to throw off Roman rule and establish political independence: the war ended with the defeat of the Jews and the destruction of Jerusalem. The last event of the war was the siege of Masada, where nearly a thousand Jews, including women and children, decided to kill themselves rather than be taken prisoner. Masada is now something of a national shrine in Israel: recruits to the army are sworn in there, and parties of schoolchildren have read out to them the story of how so many years ago Jews preferred self-inflicted death to dishonour. In the present situation in Israel, for anyone who wishes the country well, to hold up Masada as an example to be followed or equally to question, would seem to be dangerous.

The historian of the 66–73 war was Josephus; his is the only contemporary history; without it, we should know almost nothing about the war. Josephus was a Jew; he began the war as one of the Jewish commanders; after a year he went over to the Romans. For this action he has for centuries been execrated not only by Jews but by almost every commentator on the story. Yet it is his story that is read out to the schoolchildren at Masada. His words describe, with a poignancy that brings tears to the eyes, the moral grandeur of people who, when the besieging Romans were about to break into their last fortress and further resistance was useless, agreed, under their leader Eleazar, first of all to kill their loved ones — each man would kill his own wife, mother, children — then the men would draw lots to see which ten would kill the rest; then these ten would draw lots to see which one would kill the other nine; then this last one would kill himself. So that when the Romans broke in what they would find would be just the bodies of people who preferred death to dishonour; who had such a view of life that even to the Romans, thus cheated of their capture, they would seem (as Josephus says) victorious. And this story has been taken as a symbol of heroism not only by the Jews but by almost everyone who has had a feel for heroism perhaps since the invention of stories.

The reason why Josephus personally has been held in such universal contempt is not only because he went over to the Romans: it is because of his self-congratulatory style of doing and describing this. By some odd chance — or perhaps by one of those coincidences by which a story or a history are fashioned — Josephus himself, at an early stage of the war, was involved in a situation similar to that which later occurred at Masada. He was a commander of the Jewish forces in Galilee; in 67 A.D.; having fought resourcefully and bravely, he found himself besieged, hopelessly, in a town called Jotapata. Now Josephus was a young man — no more than thirty — but he came from an aristocratic background and had already been to Rome where, having been introduced to the Emperor Nero and the Empress Poppeia, he had got a taste for Roman society. He also respected Roman law and order, which he thought necessary in a world otherwise likely to be murderously chaotic. The revolt in 66 A.D. had been started by Jewish Zealots: it was Zealots who spoke of the need for national independence; yet the Romans allowed a good deal of cultural and religious freedom to Jews; and Zealots, as seems often to be the case with liberation organisations, were apt to impose their minority passions ruthlessly on a quietist majority. Josephus thought that any revolt was bound to be defeated; and that in any case Jewish interests would best be served by working with the Romans. He had tried to stop the mass of Jewish people joining the revolt; he had argued above all that it was the specific God-given role of the Jews to influence the world by the promulgation of Judaism and God's word peacefully. But his arguments had been overwhelmed by the violence of the Zealots, and the war had started. However then, as a good patriot, he had joined in, and had been placed in command of the Jewish forces in Galilee.

But when he and his men were trapped without any chance of escape in the fortress of Jotapata, it seemed to him that at least now — it is he himself, of course, who tells this story — it should be acceptable to submit to the Romans; for if the Romans had to break into the town they would almost certainly, such were the customs of warfare at the time, kill all the inhabitants including women and children; whereas if the inhabitants surrendered there would be a good chance of quite a number of them staying alive even if for a time in captivity; especially since he, Josephus, with his contacts in Rome, could intercede for them. So he put this to the townspeople — Would they not like him now to go to the Romans and arrange for them the best terms he could? But the townspeople insisted they preferred death to dishonour; and they said that if he, Josephus, was himself thinking of going over to the Romans, they would see to it that they killed him before they killed themselves.

So Josephus said that, as a good democrat, he would abide by the decision of the majority; and the next day the town was taken by the Romans.

But while the town was being sacked and the inhabitants killed Josephus did try to save himself; he went to hide in a cellar or a cave of which he knew; and there he found forty other prominent citizens who he imagined must at last be trying to save themselves; so he put it to them again — Might they not now, after they had made their gesture as it were to death rather than dishonour, let him submit to the Romans? But the citizens insisted again — No, they were hiding in the cave just so that they might carry out, on their own terms, a suicide pact; in which either he would join them, or if he did not, they would kill him. So Josephus reaffirmed he would obey the majority.

Now it is here that there is an ambiguity in the story even as told by Josephus. It was apparently agreed by the people in the cave that Josephus, as the leading citizen, should himself arrange the drawing of lots to see who should be killed by whom in the suicide pact; and it is also apparent that the drawing of lots and the killing went on until there were just two men left alive in the cave — and one of them was Josephus. In one of the versions of the story that have survived Josephus comments about his own survival — 'Shall we put it down to providence, or simply luck' — and in another he says about himself — 'He counted the numbers cunningly and so deceived them all.' It is not known which of these two versions is the more authentic: but in any case, might they not be complementary? The fact was that after a time there were just two men left alive in the cave; and Josephus put it to the other man yet again — Shall we now surrender to the Romans? And the other man said Yes.

This is the story of why Josephus has been so much hated for centuries — as being someone who, after he had done such fighting as seemed necessary, not only preferred what was traditionally called dishonour to death, but seemed openly to be somewhat mocking of the tradition about honour. And he lived to a successful old age in Italy.

It is true, is it not, that any society, if it is to hold together, has to have ideals which members of the society are ready to die for? What other sort of forces can hold a society together?

23

And it is true, is it not, that if in such circumstances an individual chooses to live, then he will naturally be seen as a traitor by those who choose to die?

All this is dependent, of course, on the belief that society is the unit that has to hold together.

But then, if the members of a society are dead, what is it that holds together?

If anything is to live, is it not individuals that do so?

But still, morally and politically, perhaps a film on such a subject should not be made.

It would be difficult for people to see it as anything other than romanticising, or mocking, the suicide of a society.

Though there were, in fact, seven people, including five children, who did survive the massacre at Masada.

And it is about them that it is conceivable, but unlikely, that a film about living could be made.

When Epstien, in the first-class compartment of the aeroplane, had read thus far in Jason's typescript, he put it down on his knee, took out a large red handkerchief, held this in front of his nose, and made against it a noise like a battering-ram.

Then he said 'You mean, you think some sort of film sympathetic to Josephus might be made?'

Jason said 'Yes.'

Epstien said 'And that would be taboo?'

Jason said 'It would be called fascist; élitist.'

'And you don't think it would be?'

'No.'

'Why not?'

Jason thought — It is now myself who-am in my town like Jotapata.

He said 'Because what is fascist and élitist is in fact, I think, making public and heroic a sort of death-wish: and what wants to stay alive is somewhat secret.'

Epstien said 'But Josephus didn't remain secret.'

Jason said 'No.'

Then he thought — Dear God, what would happen if Epstien

did make this film?

He said 'But Josephus wanted to alter the way people see things. That was why he didn't remain secret.'

Epstien said 'Alter the way that people feel that societies demand that people shall die for them?'

Jason said 'Yes.'

He thought — And I am not remaining secret?

Epstien said 'He wanted to encourage societies to live, at the cost of bringing down odium on himself?'

Jason thought — Dear God, if Epstien made such a film, would I or would I not have chosen to put myself in the position of bringing down odium on myself?

He said 'Well, it's absolutely true, of course, in the long run, morally and politically, it would be a good thing if such a film were made. I mean, if people could see the paradoxes of this sort of loyalty, this sort of death-wish — '

He thought — Dear God, what is the end of that sentence?

Epstien said ' — They wouldn't want to die?'

Jason said 'Well, they might still want to kill us!'

Epstien said 'But would it not be part of your argument that societies have to hold together, even if in some sense die, in order that individuals might have a chance to live even if secretly?'

Jason thought — That really is clever!

He said 'Yes: but that's too dangerous now.'

He thought — But with Epstien cross-examining me like a lawyer, it is of course unlikely that he will make this film.

Epstien said 'You mean, individuals who want to live can no longer remain hidden?'

Jason said 'If society blows itself up, all individuals are taken along with it.'

Epstien said 'So the values of the individuals have to be made public — '

Jason said 'They might envy us: they wouldn't kill us.'

Epstien flapped the typescript up and down on his knee.

He said 'And now how would you get out of your town like Jotapata?'

Jason thought — It's true, yes, that it's not just a question of

25

staying alive: it's a question of how to live with having done this —

He said 'It's a question of the way you see things: a style.'

Epstien said 'You think there's a style in which you could make this film?'

Jason said 'Possibly.'

Epstien said 'What?'

Jason said 'I think it would be to do with what goes on in your mind: with what you know is acting; and the part of you which knows this, which is not.'

Epstien said 'Acting — '

Jason said 'I mean, it depends on the distinction between what you pretend, to stay alive; and what you live with, which is real.'

Epstien said 'You could pretend to accept the values of a society?'

Jason said 'Yes. If this was what its members thought they wanted from you.'

Epstien said 'And you think they'd believe you?'

Jason said 'If they wanted — '

'And you'd let them — '

'Let them what?'

'Die.'

Jason said 'But you'd be trying to save them.'

Epstien said 'How?'

Jason said 'I think, just by demonstrating that it's the fact that you know what has to be pretended, and not what is pretended, which is real.'

He thought — Dear God, I do see it was difficult for those citizens of Jotapata!

Epstien banged the typescript up and down on his knee.

He said 'Look: this is the story of a man who has a high opinion of himself: who wants to stay alive: who does not mind if others die. You think you can do this without offending society?'

Jason said 'No.' Then — 'That's what I've said.'

He thought — What you mean is, I can't say it without offending you.

26

Then — I am like Daniel in the lions' den.

He said 'Society might still thank you.'

Epstien said 'Secretly!'

Jason said 'Yes.'

Epstien laughed.

Jason said 'It's true for the most part now that people who are publicly successful protect themselves by making themselves out to be failures gloriously — '

Epstien said 'Failures gloriously?'

Jason said 'Films are traditionally about how to be failures gloriously: how to be loved because of this.'

Epstien said ' — You're either hated and secretly respected, or loved and are a failure gloriously — ?'

Jason said 'Yes.'

Epstien said 'And you think the Jews have a special role in all this?'

Jason thought — Ah, this is the area in which, traditionally, one is defeated at Jotapata!

He said 'Well, I think the Jews have a special role in lots of things: but they seem better able than most to live with paradoxes.'

Epstien said 'How?'

Jason said 'They make jokes.'

Epstien said 'And you think that is the style in which they survive?'

Jason thought — Or do not survive?

He said 'But you see, one has to become more conscious of what one is doing in making jokes.'

For some time he had been watching the back of the head of the man in the seat on the right of the aisle in front. He could see just one side of the head, where the dark hair was cut neatly and precisely. He thought — Can one tell a film star by his hair being cut like one of those birds or animals out of hedges?

Epstien said 'Conscious of the role between the individual and society?'

Jason said 'Conscious of what an individual and society are.'

Epstien said 'And this is to do with acting?'

Jason was thinking — Can one tell an actor by himself being

so conscious of being watched that he is like that painting of a man seen from the back looking into a mirror and seeing his head from the back —

Epstien, beside him, suddenly called out — 'Wolf, do you think films are about how to be failures gloriously?'

Jason wanted to say — But I've just said acting might be a means of showing people how to stay alive!

The head of the man in the seat on the right in front was coming round: first the profile, the fine-drawn nose, the skin like soft leather; then the bright blue eyes, the famous smile that went up higher on one side than the other —

'We haven't been introduced.'

Epstien said 'Jason. Mr Wolf Tanner.'

Jason said 'How do you do.'

Wolf Tanner said ' — Films are about how to be failures gloriously?'

Jason said 'I was saying they might show a style of something to do with how to live — '

Wolf Tanner said ' — How to live — '

Jason thought — Ah, yes, because you can hypnotise people; with your bright blue eyes, your way of repeating things as if your eyebrows were inverted commas —

He said 'Acting can be a protection.'

Wolf Tanner said 'Against what?'

Jason said 'Envy. Power.'

Wolf Tanner stared at him. He said 'The envy of people who don't want to live — '

Jason said 'Yes.'

He thought — What is this about? I've forgotten —

Then Wolf Tanner said 'I hear you've got a beautiful wife.'

IV

In the tourist-class compartment of the aeroplane Lilia was almost sure she had heard what the man beside her had said: he had said 'I have got sweeties' and she had said 'What?' and he had said 'Can you help me?' But the whole thing had been so quiet she could not be sure. She thought — One's mind plays tricks; lets one hear what one wants; or is it he who is playing tricks? Or why might I want to hear this? The man had continued to clutch his stomach as if in pain. Lilia sat with her eyes closed. Then when the plane had been in the air some time the man suddenly stood and went lurching down the aisle towards the lavatories at the back. She thought — But the lights are still on telling us to fasten our seat-belts; he is so desperate he has had to go to give himself a fix; or he will come bursting out with his guns and bombs and things and will demand to be flown to Zanzibar or somewhere; such is the plight of people who have to rush to lavatories on planes. He had left his bag on the seat beside her. She thought — Perhaps now I can look inside it; but would he have left it if it contains a bomb? or perhaps he has got remote control or something —

Her child said 'What that's ticking — '

She said 'Ticking!'

Her child said 'Sticking!'

The child was moving his fingers round the top of the cup in which she had given him orange juice.

She thought — But the man cannot be going to blow up a plane he's in unless it's for insurance for his wife and he doesn't look the sort of man who's got a wife; or unless he can get out of the lavatory by parachute or something; but I don't think you can, can you, unless you get yourself sucked out of a very small hole like that man in that film what was its name —

Then — They are like shadows on a wall, these images?

Poking out of the top of the bag on the seat was the man's bottle of whisky. She thought — I could take a quick swig and then fill it up again and put it back: but how could I fill it up if it's the man who's in the lavatory —

Then — Really, if our minds are dominated by these sorts of images —

Her child said 'Mummy — '

She said 'Yes?'

'Where's that man gone?'

'He's gone to pee.'

'He's not gone to pee.'

'What do you think he's doing then?'

Her child looked at her solemnly; then began to roll about with laughter.

She thought — Really, this can't be the sort of thing that gets children into the kingdom of heaven.

She picked up Jason's typescript again. She laid aside the first few pages which were fastened separately and which she had already read. She began to read where the typing was in the form of a filmscript.

Josephus, as a young man in Palestine, has gone to live with a hermit called Bannus in the desert. Bannus was once an Essene: Essenes were people who withdrew from society and lived in communes. But Bannus has withdrawn further, and is a hermit.

SCENE: the desert. The pale blue mountains of Judaea are in the background.

Bannus squats in the dust. He draws on the ground with a stick.

Josephus, aged about twenty, squats facing him. They wear goat-skins.

When Josephus speaks it is as if he does not expect any answer.

JOSEPHUS

— He died —

— He came alive —

Bannus draws in the dust.

JOSEPHUS

He'd been dead for three days.

How did he come alive?

That's what's interesting.

Bannus stops drawing. He has made a pattern that does not seem to mean anything.

JOSEPHUS

He can't just have got up.

That would be boring.

— I say, bet you can't do this —

That would be a miracle.

Bannus looks up.

JOSEPHUS

I mean, the whole idea would be boring —

You could either do it or you couldn't.

Bannus looks away to the mountains of Judaea.

JOSEPHUS

Of course you want to die for the sake of other people. It cheers them up. And you feel powerful. But what's the point of that if you're dead? Naturally, you want to come alive again —

Bannus looks at him.

JOSEPHUS

And then you can watch all those people you've died for, given something to live for, worshipping you —

Bannus hits at the ground in front of Josephus with his stick.

JOSEPHUS

All right, all right —

He watches Bannus. He seems to quote —

JOSEPHUS

— O death, where is thy sting —

Bannus smiles at him.

Josephus lies on his back and puts his hands beneath his head.

JOSEPHUS

When I was at school, we studied Plato. Plato said that there were ideas that were more real than experience, because the way in which experience was known depended on them. So in order to understand experience, we had to understand ideas: but how could we understand ideas if the only things we had to understand them by were ideas —

He glances at Bannus who is looking away to the mountains.

JOSEPHUS

It's a matter of language.

Language is a mirror.

Why do you never speak?

You look like — a metaphor.

Bannus smiles at him.

Josephus looks up at the sky.

JOSEPHUS

When we were at school, we did the story of the Tower of Babel. Men had all one language, and were building a tower to be equal to gods. So God became jealous, and confused men's languages. But what was the language that men had, when they were becoming equal to gods?

He looks at Bannus.

Bannus is smiling.

JOSEPHUS

We're sitting in a cave, watching shadows cast on a wall. But if we know they're shadows, we know there's a sun.

Bannus does not move.

JOSEPHUS

Silence? Listening?

Bannus holds out the stick to him.

JOSEPHUS

That we know we're all metaphors —

That is the sun?

Bannus remains holding out the stick.

JOSEPHUS

— What is dead comes alive —

He reaches as if for the stick.

32

Bannus takes the stick back.
Josephus remains with his hand out.

> JOSEPHUS

—It was the serpent in the Garden of Eden who said —
I can make you superior to gods —

Bannus looks round as if for somewhere to throw the stick.

> JOSEPHUS

— Gods have such a terrible life after all: making everyone want to kill them: only coming alive again after the third act —

Bannus looks at him.

> JOSEPHUS

Like kings: like princes. Like pictures stuck on a wall —
He leans forward and takes the stick from Bannus.

> JOSEPHUS

What was that first bird that Noah sent out of the ark?
— Go on: fetch it —

He throws the stick away.
He looks into the camera.
When Bannus speaks, he seems obviously to be acting.

> BANNUS

— I say, when are you going to Rome? —
Josephus lies back and looks up at the sky.

> JOSEPHUS

— All the world's a stage —
Who said that?

> BANNUS

— You can learn one or two things there you know! —

> JOSEPHUS

The bird never returned.
It flew round and round, for ever.
He looks into the camera.

> JOSEPHUS

I see.
No I don't.

Bannus watches him.

JOSEPHUS
They'll try to kill me?
He stands up and prances round flapping his arms up and
down like a bird.
Then he stops and looks at Bannus.
JOSEPHUS
We know we're metaphors —

At this point Lilia, in the tourist compartment of the aeroplane, put the typescript down on her knee and said to herself
— Dear God! You didn't really think, did you, anyone would
make a film of this?
Then she read —

JOSEPHUS
It's a joke?
That'll kill them?

Lilia thought — What has happened: you've become like
Josephus, you want to kill people?
Then — We know we're metaphors?
She became aware that someone was standing in the aisle
beside her: it was the man who had returned from the lavatory.
She found herself covering up the typescript with her hand.
She thought — Is it so secret then?
The man settled down again in the seat beside her. He still
seemed to be ill, but in an even more urgent way. His mouth
was wide open and he had a hand down by his groin. He
breathed quickly. She thought — His fix has not worked? his
needle has got stuck in his —
Then — I really must ask him: Are you all right?
— For if everything is a metaphor, then we can live with this
sort of thing, can't we, O Jason?
She did nothing for a time. She seemed to doze.
— She was again in a hot room in a hotel in the desert:
there was a bed, a chair, a wash-stand between windows —
She thought — Does it make it any better if we know these
images come from our unconscious?

Then she said 'Are you all right?'

The man said 'No.'

She said 'Why not?'

She thought — I am like Bannus: or he is like Bannus: in the dust, in the desert —

Then — The point of these images is, isn't it, if we see them, we see ourselves —

— And in so doing, we are not like them?

The man said 'I'm in agony!'

She said 'Why?'

She thought — Those drops of sweat on his forehead are like pricks from thorns —

Then — Oh really!

The man groaned.

There was a coming and going of hostesses through the curtain to the first-class. She thought — They will be getting their champagne and caviare and things —

The man said again 'Will you help me?'

She said 'How?'

She thought — Because this, you see, is the question that is not boring.

She looked at her child who seemed to be asleep beside her.

She thought — What was that picture of Mary and Joseph and the infant Jesus crossing a desert on a donkey —

The man said 'Please!'

She said 'I'll call the steward.'

He said 'No.'

She said 'Why not?'

She thought — Well of course, if he has got a needle stuck in his —

— Or dope or diamonds up his —

— Can I help him?

The man said 'Will you come with me to the back of the plane?'

She said 'No of course not!'

He said 'Why?'

She thought — Oh God, that smell: that small hot room in the desert —

She looked round as if she might find some pattern in the dust to help her.

She said 'I've got my child.'

— That taste of iron on the tongue: a root coming out of the earth to fill her —

She said 'What do you want me to do?'

He said 'I want you to help me.'

She thought — I might ask the hostess to keep an eye on my child.

She found she was shaking.

She said 'Wait.'

She thought — Dear God, but do you not say, O Jason, do what you want, if you want to find out what is true?

Then — This feeling of sweetness is like a bird coming down —

The man said 'Thank you!'

She thought — A snake that is turning to the sun is true?

V

Wolf Tanner, in the first-class compartment of the aeroplane, exclaimed — 'For God's sake, let's have some champagne!'

When Jason had first come into the compartment it had seemed that both Wolf Tanner and the not-quite-so-famous actress in the seat beside him were asleep. Or perhaps they were drugged, Jason had thought: being famous, might not they, like Epstien, have some eccentricity such as being frightened of travelling on planes? The steward and the two air hostesses had moved past them gingerly, giving them sidelong glances every now and then as if not wanting to be caught peeping at Lady Godiva. Then Wolf Tanner had stirred, and there had been a flurry of activity: drinks were wheeled in on a trolley: behind, there was a clatter of food being prepared.

Jason thought — A first-class compartment is like a 1930s play about Mount Olympus.

Wolf Tanner, watching champagne being poured into his glass, said 'Hoo—ray and up she rises!'

Epstien said 'If one must be a failure, let one be a failure gloriously — '

Wolf Tanner said 'This is a far, far better Krug '72 — '

Jason thought — Was it the oddity of their own conversation that made gods jealous of men building their tower towards heaven?

Epstien had not read any further in the script.

Jason said to Wolf Tanner 'Would you like to look at these outlines of scenes that I've done?'

Wolf Tanner said 'You're not allowed to ask a direct question!'

He ran his finger round the top of his glass as if he could make it sing; then dabbed his finger behind his ear.

Jason said to Epstien 'Josephus was a writer. He must have

known that what he was doing would bring down odium on himself.'

Wolf Tanner said 'Oh dee-um oh dee-um!'

Jason thought — Well, that's witty.

Epstien said 'Why?'

Wolf Tanner said 'Lose two turns.'

Jason watched his glass being filled. He thought — People imagine they might feel at home in heaven, because bubbles come up from the hell of their unconscious?

He said 'It might have made things easier for him.'

Epstien said 'What?'

Wolf Tanner said 'Next question.'

Jason said 'Being thought a shit.'

Epstien said 'Would have made what easier?'

Jason said 'Then he wouldn't feel responsible any more.'

Wolf Tanner said 'Right.'

Jason said 'Now can I ask a direct question?'

Wolf Tanner said 'Isn't that the direct question?'

His blue eyes stared at Jason. Jason thought — They are like smart bright swimming-pools.

He said 'As an actor, you might see what my script's about.'

Wolf Tanner said 'That's not a question.'

Jason thought — In that blue and sterilised water, a child might have drowned.

He said 'The point of acting is, isn't it, to feel not responsible but still be popular.'

Wolf Tanner said 'Yes, I will look at your script.'

Jason said 'Right.'

He took hold of the lower and bulkier part of the typescript on Epstien's knee. Epstien held on to the other side of it as if he were a child.

Jason thought — This tug-of-war is by the swimming-pool in which the child might have drowned?

He let go of his end of the script.

The hostess was leaning over the two people at the back. She said 'Would you like some champagne?'

Wolf Tanner said 'With beaded bubbles winking at the bum.' He had leaned round and was staring at the hostess' back.

The hostess began to laugh so much that she had to retire behind the curtain by the steward's cabin still holding the champagne.

Jason said 'You have to make out you're awful so people can love you, and not be envious any more.'

Wolf Tanner said 'But you have not to be awful?'

Jason said 'No.'

Wolf Tanner said ' — Who will rid me of this turbulent priest — '

Jason said 'Exactly.'

He thought — Can I explain that it is to do with language: jumping from one level to another —

Then — In those smart bright swimming-pools, the child might yet come alive?

He said 'But how are you not awful — '

Wolf Tanner said 'That is the question!'

Jason thought — You watch yourself? as something moving between levels?

He said 'What do you think you're doing when you act?'

Wolf Tanner said 'Getting people to love me.'

Jason said 'But if you know — '

He thought, staring at Wolf Tanner — The difference between homosexual love and heterosexual love is that with homosexual love you can do what you like and still be respected by the other person?

He had an image, suddenly, of a hotel room in the desert: a bed, a chair, a wash-stand between windows —

Epstien, on Jason's left, had for some time been trying to swivel round in his seat to attract the hostess' attention and get some more champagne. The hostess reappeared with a new bottle. She seemed to have put more make-up on her face. She re-filled Epstien's glass.

Then Epstien said loudly 'I don't want to make a film about people making witty remarks! I want to make a film about flesh and blood!'

Wolf Tanner held out his glass and intoned ' — We do not presume to come to this thy table, O Lord — '

The hostess looked as if she might have to go behind the

curtain again.

Jason said 'I don't think flesh and blood are the most interesting parts of people.'

He thought — Wolf Tanner and I could do a successful cross-talk act: he would be the funny straight man, and I the heavy comic.

A second hostess had come in with a tray of food. She was trying to put it in front of Wolf Tanner. Wolf Tanner raised his hands above his head and made a terrified face and said 'Clang!' Then — 'Home, James, and don't spare the bondage.'

The second hostess began to laugh so much she had to go through the door to the captain's cabin.

Epstien said 'What I want is facts. There are plenty of facts about Palestine and Rome in the first century A.D.'

Wolf Tanner sang ' — Facts, facts, lovely juicy facts — '

Jason began to laugh. He thought — What is magical, is when what you are talking about begins to happen at the same time.

Wolf Tanner sang ' — In the stores, in the stores — '

Jason said 'There were, yes, a lot of interesting things going on — '

He thought — Of course, were not Wolf Tanner and Epstien once lovers?

Epstien said 'The facts are that Roman rule was oppressive. The fact is that oppressed people want their freedom.'

Wolf Tanner sang ' — Nats, nats, lovely juicy nats — '

Trays with caviare and smoked salmon were being put in front of Epstien and Jason. Jason thought — O Lilia, you'll never forgive me!

He said 'But the most interesting thing was the struggle between people who wanted to be told what to do, who always had been told what to do, by gods or rulers or their unconscious or whatever; and those people who wanted to find out what they wanted to do themselves, and do it.'

Wolf Tanner sang ' — In the province of Galilee! — '

Then he leaned round and stared again at Jason.

He said ' — And stay alive.'

Jason said 'And stay alive.'

'And the other people wanted to die?'

'Obedient people are those who are ready to die — '

' — And they would try to stop the others staying alive?'

Jason thought — Now, yes, does what is drowned come alive?

Epstien, beside him, had eaten several biscuits with caviare very quickly; he had pushed smoked salmon into his mouth as if it were a gag; now he lifted his tray and seemed to be looking for somewhere to get rid of it.

Jason said 'The people who wanted to obey, to be ready to die, always in a sense won. Perhaps they had to win — a church, an empire — for law and order.'

Wolf Tanner said 'And what happened to the others?'

Jason said 'They hid. Or acted.'

'Or were killed — '

' — Or were they acting?'

Epstien said 'Steward, can I have two brandies?'

He was trying to balance his tray on the top of the seat in front of him.

Wolf Tanner sang quietly ' — Brands, brands, lovely burning brandies — '

Epstien said 'Be careful, Wolf!'

Wolf Tanner sang ' — On the bum, on the bum — '

Jason thought — In fact, is there some quite different battle going on —

— They had orgies in Rome?

Then Wolf Tanner said 'And what about the Jews?'

Jason said 'They were defeated. They stayed alive. They got themselves scattered. They proliferated.'

He remembered — But what they spread would be about defeat —

He wanted to say — But you must read my script!

Epstien, with a push of his finger, sent the tray over the top of the seat in front of him. It bounced, and scattered, the bread and salad going on to the floor.

Jason thought — Now I must try to get hold of something in all this: when I first came in it was Epstien I had to talk to, to say what I had to say about the script, however clumsy, however unsayable. And Epstien seemed interested for a time: perhaps this was only to blow hot and cold. Then the cold was when he brought in Wolf Tanner. But this went quite well for a time. Then — Was it when I again said something about the Jews?

— But I have said only good things about Jews!

— Is it this that is unbearable?

Epstien had pushed his seat back as far as it would go, and was lying with his huge stomach almost horizontal.

One of the hostesses had come up and was trying to pick up the food from the floor.

Jason thought — Epstien is or is not a Jew? Wolf Tanner is or is not a Jew? But this is not the point —

— If Epstien is God the Father; and Wolf Tanner, as actor with two personalities, is God the Son —

He tried to remember what he had heard of Epstien and Wolf Tanner when he had worked with Epstien in Rome. Wolf Tanner was homosexual: Epstien was homosexual? or was he bisexual: he had some peculiarity to do with —

Then he thought — It is true there is nothing interesting in all this: but what is interesting is almost impossible to hold in mind.

He wanted to say to no one in particular — You see, the reason why fighting and being ready to die is easier than living is because for dying you have everything laid out as if it were a head on a platter —

— And for living, you're flying above the sea for ever and have to find your own way —

— It is that bird that flew out of the ark, which people are always forgetting?

For some time there had been signs of movement from the seat on Wolf Tanner's right. Here, Jason had guessed, there was the not-quite-so-famous film actress who he had been told would also be on the plane. Now, over the top of the chair like some cartoon of the rising sun, there came a nimbus of smooth fair hair, then the lenses of enormous dark glasses, then a rather flat, crumpled face like a shape waiting to have adornment put on it.

The face said 'Did I hear brandy?'

42

Jason thought — But it is I who am that bird, looking at these faces as if for somewhere to land?

Then — I must not be blasphemous.

Wolf Tanner said 'The Empress Poppeia riseth from her bath!'

Jason thought — But he can't, can he, have been reading my script?

The face said 'We haven't been introduced.'

Wolf Tanner said 'Miss Lisa Grant.'

Jason said 'Hullo.'

Lisa Grant said 'I want to read your script.'

Wolf Tanner said 'Epstien has impounded all the scripts — '

Lisa Grant said 'Why?'

Wolf Tanner said ' — As if they were stories of Miss Stalin and the Polish Schoolgirls.'

Jason said 'Here.' He bent down to his bag and produced another typescript out of it.

He thought — This is the last of my poor orphaned scripts!

Epstien said 'I don't want anyone to read that script!'

Lisa Grant said 'What is it about this script?'

Wolf Tanner said 'Abracadabra!'

Jason said 'Exactly.'

Epstien said 'I've paid for it. It's my script!'

Wolf Tanner said 'It has to be circulated underground secretly.'

Jason held out the typescript to Wolf Tanner. Wolf Tanner took it and made as if to hold it out to Lisa Grant. Lisa Grant made as if to take it; then Wolf Tanner snatched it back and held it to his heart and made a face like a startled clown.

Lisa Grant said 'I don't think I can bear this.'

Wolf Tanner said 'You can bear anything, darling, if you start slowly enough.'

Lisa Grant turned and kneeled on her seat and seemed about to try to climb over the back of it.

Wolf Tanner leaned sideways and put his arms round her and kissed her behind.

Lisa Grant said 'Where's your partner, darling?'

Wolf Tanner said 'In the tourist.'

Lisa Grant said 'Is he always in the tourist?'

Wolf Tanner said 'Except when the tourist is in him.'

Then he leaned the other way into the aisle and made his bright clown's face with his mouth in an O.

A hostess came up with two glasses of brandy. Epstien took one and Lisa Grant took the other.

Wolf Tanner sat back and opened Jason's typescript.

Jason thought — Behind those eyes, the child will not come alive?

Then — But you are all right, my Lilia?

VI

When, after a time, Lilia got up and went with the dark-skinned man to the back of the plane she thought — I am mad: he may — what? in fact rape me? have a gun or something and stick it in my back? put his arm round my throat and turn to the steward or captain and say — Fly this aeroplane to Libya or Zanzibar or somewhere; and I will be staring out above his arm with wild terrified eyes and my skirt drawn tight above my knees as in some film about bad housing conditions in Glasgow or Liverpool or somewhere. The man was waiting for her by the semi-circle of lavatory doors. She was still in her fantasy — And then I will be made to walk ahead of him across some tarmac and the eyes of the world will be upon me through television and when I reach the airport building there will be that noise like a sneeze behind me and the gasp of the crowd and I will be going at the knees with a bullet in my back and the darkness coming down on me —

The man said 'You go in first.' She said 'No you go in first.' She thought — This is ridiculous. All the lavatories seemed occupied. If the man did take out a gun how long would it be, she wondered, before anyone came to rescue her? would her child wake up and start calling? could she get through to Jason by telepathy? She and Jason had tried this sort of thing once or twice on long winter evenings; but Jason had said — . The man waiting with her seemed again to be in pain or to be acting; he had doubled up and was holding on to his groin. Jason had said — But in pain it's a help to act; you make it more bearable. But what had he said about telepathy? She wondered — But if this man has got a needle stuck in wherever it is, surely he can get it out? unless it's like a fish hook. What Jason had said was — I don't know if telepathy's true, but it's true that some people are more likely to be thinking the same things at the same time

45

than others. She thought — And God is like a fish hook. Then — Jason used to say that? There was an old woman coming out of one of the lavatories; the man was making a gesture for her to go in. She thought — Of course, we already seem to be doing something improper: what is it about sex and lavatories? It was God, didn't someone say, who put them so close together? She went into the lavatory; the man was squeezing in behind her. She thought — What was that film where dozens of people all get into a ship's cabin, or a telephone box, or something: now why is that funny? The man was having difficulty in closing the door. It seemed as if she would have to climb up on to the seat as women are supposed to do when a mouse is after them; and then she might be sucked out through the plug like that man in — what was that film called? Well, that was funny. The man had managed to close the door; Lilia turned and sat down on the seat. The man was almost on top of her. She thought she might say — Now what is all this? like a headmistress, with a man in a lavatory almost on top of her. She said 'Now what is all this?' The man began to undo the belt of his trousers. She thought — For goodness' sake, spin it out a little bit, can't you? The man said 'A ring.' She said 'A ring?' She thought — A wedding ring? a Wagnerian ring? the ring at the end of a piggy-wig's nose? She said 'What do you mean, a ring?' The man was taking down his trousers. She thought — Oh well, at least this is one way of doing it. She frowned. She thought — I must appear impassive. Then — But isn't it supposed to be more exciting when you pretend it's something different? The man said 'It's agony!' She thought — Doctors and nurses! then you can imagine you're helping suffering humanity. The man did in fact seem to have a ring, or something, just above, or below, the end of his penis. She thought — Depending on which way you look at it: or it looks at you, up or down, ha ha, isn't that funny. She found she did want to giggle. The ring was cutting into the man's flesh quite deeply. She thought — He can't get the ring off because he has an erection and he has an erection because he can't get the ring off; this is what Jason calls a double-bind: the tie put upon one by society. Then — That's something to do with circumcision, isn't it? Why are men circumcised, do you know?

46

She said 'How did it get there?' She thought — I know men are circumcised in order not to get sand in it in the desert and things like that, but why religiously? It was a gold ring, a little wider than a wedding ring: she wondered if she could take hold of it gently. She thought — Men are circumcised because by pain they are tethered to society? He said 'My friend put it there.' She thought — With friends like that — ! Then — And so people are tethered to love? to friendship? She found she could in fact now take hold of his penis gently. She thought — Well, this does seem to work: what does it matter whether or not he is acting? She felt, as she had done once or twice before in her life, as if she were holding some root that went down into the earth; that was also holding her by the throat. She thought — Sexuality forms a circuit: to the sun, and so round beyond the back wall of the cave. Then — Now who was thinking that? She said 'Why did your friend put it there?' He said 'I don't know.' She said 'You must.' She thought — But all this is a game; I must remember: some thread through to my own bi-sexuality. Beyond the back wall of the cave. The ring seemed to have a sort of hinge at the top and on the underneath a built-in lock, very finely made, as if by a jeweller. She thought — Well, your friend must be rich. The man said 'I suppose it was to keep me faithful.' She thought — Well, your friend's a fool. Then — But being circumcised is not the same as being castrated, is it? The man's penis was large and swollen: it bulged at the end beyond the ring like the pod of a tropical flower. She said 'Well can't you put it under a cold tap or something?' He said 'No I've tried that.' She thought — This is ridiculous. Then — I suppose he wants me to put it in my mouth. The man's penis was an inch or two from her face. She thought — I am large, I contain multitudes. Then — Now who was thinking that? She said 'Well what can I do?' He said 'Oh help me!' She thought — Yes, that's right. She thought she was going to faint. There seemed to be a sort of smell in the confined space that dogs must have when they sniff at arses. She said 'And you haven't got the key.' He said 'No I haven't got the key.' She thought — Oh well, what more can I say. She put the penis in her mouth. She thought she might say — Does that make it any

47

better? But she couldn't speak. She was his mother and he was her baby. Or he was her mother and she was his baby. She could bite his penis off, or her breast off, and destroy him. Or her. What do psychiatrists say about this? — And watch the seeds from the castrated seed-pod fly away over the world. But you have to work at this, psychiatrists say, don't you? When you are feeding your baby. When what is soft is protected by a hard band between the teeth. When all roles are reversible in this actors' world. Fly away, fly away, seed-pod. She bit with her lips. Her mind went blank. There was the effusion of the game, the maze: the secret at the centre of the flower.

After a time, when Lilia felt she could breathe again, there seemed to be someone knocking on the door of the lavatory.

She thought — My child! Or the police trying to break in, with axes.

The man said 'Don't go!'

She had some vision of his hitting her on the back of her head and killing her.

She thought — Ah, but the pistol has been to the roof of my mouth —

— Where can I spit the bullets out?

The man said 'I've got a gun.'

She thought — This is ridiculous.

The man said 'Do as I tell you.'

Cold air seemed to be coming in. The snake was trying to lie curled up at the bottom of the tree. Her surroundings had a different light on them.

There was a banging again on the outside of the door of the lavatory and then a voice — 'Will you return to your seats please.'

Lilia removed her head. There was the man just in front of her, like ashes.

She thought — Really, he is rather beautiful: small now, and wrinkled like roses.

The voice from outside said 'There's been a complaint.'

Lilia thought she might say — But you are comfy?

It was now quite easy to take the ring off.

The voice from outside said 'I must ask you to come out

immediately.'

Lilia wiped her face with the end of the man's shirt.

He said 'I had the key all the time.'

She thought — Of course you did.

Then — But you don't want to show me how all your tricks are done, do you?

It was an expertly made ring; like a small pair of false teeth.

She looked up at him. She thought — But he has changed. There is a glitter now in his eyes as if he has put on make-up.

There was the banging on the door again.

Lilia said 'I could say I've been giving you an injection.'

She tried to stand up; then she had to sit down again.

She thought — What would he do if, before we went out, I kissed him?

He said 'How could you say you have been giving me an injection?'

She said 'I've been a nurse.'

He was doing up his trousers. On the backs of his hands there were bruises like ink.

She thought — He is in fact a junkie?

He said 'Do you know who I am?'

She said 'No.'

She thought — You mean, you're famous?

He said 'You don't know my boyfriend?'

She thought — Oh, a boyfriend —

He said 'What if I tell him — '

She said 'Tell him what?'

She thought — I am sad he has a boyfriend, because I thought I might see him again?

Then — But what was touched, was my bisexuality?

He said 'What we've been doing.'

She said 'What have we been doing?'

She thought — For, as Jason would say, you make it up anyway, don't you —

— With your small boy's face: your hair like down, not even feathers —

He said 'Hey!'

She had stood up and had pressed her cheek against his

49

shoulder.

He said 'You're very cool, aren't you?'

Then they had to squeeze against each other to open the door. She thought — Are all sexual games like getting into or out of lavatories?

Then — Do I not have thoughts just like yours, O Jason!

Outside there was the space within the semicircle of lavatory doors and the hostess and the old woman who had been in the lavatory before them standing like the Eumenides. She thought — Or like football players at a throw-in —

Lilia said 'I'm a nurse. I've been giving him an injection.'

Then she began walking up the aisle.

She thought — Oh you can get away with anything, can't you, if you play nurses and doctors.

Then — But my child, he is still sleeping?

The hostess and the old woman were following her up the aisle.

She thought — You old harpies, you think you know about power?

Then when she got to her row of seats her child was not there. She had left him sleeping by the window. She had asked the hostess to watch him. Now she turned back down the aisle and faced the hostess and the old woman with eyes that she was sure were blazing, and she said 'Where is my child?'

The hostess said 'We had this complaint.'

She said 'I don't care about your complaint! I asked you to look after my child.'

She thought — Fart at them: hold a crucifix out to them: you can defeat them with a child.

The hostess said 'He said he went to look out for his daddy.'

Lilia thought — Oh I do see, yes, this is all rather complicated for the hostess.

She said 'And did he know where his daddy was?'

The hostess said 'Yes, he's in the first-class.'

Lilia thought — So this has all worked quite well, hasn't it, O Jason.

The hostess said 'He is a very determined little boy.'

Lilia smiled and said 'Yes he is, isn't he.'

The man has come up the aisle and was waiting for her to go in to her seat. She thought — But there's still a danger, isn't there, if you use children?

She went to the seat by the window and picked up the picture book, the fire-engine —

She said as if to her child — Oh please forgive me —

The dark-haired man was trying to get into the seat beside her. Lilia put the picture book and the fire-engine on the seat.

Then she thought — When I put my head against his shoulder it was as if he might cry?

The man settled down in the seat by the aisle. He shook his head. He was screwing a bit of paper up between his fingers.

Lilia said 'What's wrong with you now?'

She thought — He might be taking dope as well as what we did in the lavatory?

Then — Well I can't do any more, can I?

She picked up Jason's typescript. It flopped open at a page —

She thought — My child is not in danger? Then — But one needs all the help one can get.

She read —

POPPEIA
    Why are Jews circumcised, do you know?

She thought — One is helped by coincidences?

— Some people are in fact more likely to be thinking the same thing at the same time than others?

She put the typescript down.

She said 'Why are you circumcised, do you know?'

The man beside her almost shouted 'No!'

She said 'But don't you ever ask?'

The man's face, when she watched it, was like something she might have got pleasure from by hurting it.

She said 'I just think it's extraordinary that men never ask.'

She picked up the typescript again.

The man said 'Don't you feel degraded?'

She said 'Oh God, do I feel degraded!'

She put the typescript down.

She rested her head back and closed her eyes. She imagined her child going into the first-class compartment and finding Jason. The child would have said 'Daddy!' and then would have begun laughing with his bright, dark eyes.

The man said 'You knew all the time I'd got the key? I'd only just put the ring on?'

She said 'I thought you were a hijacker.'

He said 'But you came with me?'

She said 'No, I suppose I made that up. As an excuse.'

He said 'An excuse for what?'

She thought — To come with you.

She said 'It was like your ring.'

She thought — And all forms of social activity.

He said 'What was like my ring?'

She said 'We had to have an act.'

He said 'You like to be degraded?'

She thought she might say — Oh well, we all like sometimes to be degraded —

— It makes us feel at home —

— The question is, do we admit this and get pleasure, or do we have guilt and destroy things.

She said 'You're such a puritan.'

He said 'You're doing this as some sort of joke?'

She held the typescript. She began to read.

She thought — But we know all about this, don't we, O Jason?

VII

SCENE: Rome, 64 A.D. Josephus, in his mid-twenties, is
walking in the street with Aliturus, an actor.
When Aliturus talks it is sometimes as if he were acting,
sometimes as if he were acting that he were not.

ALITURUS

He says he wants to be an actor. The Emperor! But
don't be taken in by this. He really does want to be an
actor. Has someone said that? They will, they will —
He stops and puts his hand on his heart and rolls his eyes.
Then they walk on.

ALITURUS

He'd been playing Orestes. The Emperor Nero. Now
everyone loves Orestes. Orestes murdered his mother —
He stops and acts —

ALITURUS

— Mother: you flung me to a life of pain! —
He speaks in his ordinary voice —

ALITURUS

Well, she did, actually. His mother.
The Emperor's mother.
So — Are we the same person?
They walk on.

ALITURUS

Does life imitate art?
If not, why do we do it?
We like to look at ourselves?
So the Emperor Nero murdered his mother.
He stops and seems to think.

ALITURUS

There are all those screams off stage. People like seeing
things about people murdering their mothers. It

53

cheers them up.

Most of them want to, I suppose.

And so on and so on.

They walk on.

JOSEPHUS

And did it?

ALITURUS

What?

JOSEPHUS

Cheer them up.

ALITURUS *

Oh yes, he's a very indulgent Emperor. It was all the
rage for days —

He stops and acts —

ALITURUS

— Did you hear what he did to her? —

He seems to recite —

ALITURUS

— He sent her to sea in a sieve he did —

— In a sieve he sent her to sea —

They walk on. He speaks in his ordinary voice —

ALITURUS

Someone should write a song about that.

Perhaps they will.

But she could swim.

So they had to have a re-write.

He stops and acts —

ALITURUS

— Is this a dagger that I see before me —

He says in his ordinary voice —

ALITURUS

Well, it isn't, actually.

But then — it was!

Is the difference important?

These are philosophical questions.

They walk on.

JOSEPHUS

But still people liked it —

ALITURUS

Oh yes. But not the critics, you see.

The critics, they like the unities of — time, place, illusion —

Aliturus and Josephus go through a doorway from the street into a riding school or gymnasium. There are boys and girls in short white tunics. At the far end is a platform with a semicircle of pillars so that it is like a small stage, or temple. Here are Nero and Poppeia, the Emperor and Empress. He is in his mid-twenties: she is slightly older. He is dressed as a woman: she as a boy. They are studying a scroll which Poppeia is holding.

Josephus and Aliturus stand at the back watching.

JOSEPHUS

And now he wants to die —

ALITURUS

To be able to come alive again —

JOSEPHUS

Why?

ALITURUS

To have a bit of peace.

JOSEPHUS

But the court at Athens cleared him —

ALITURUS

Who, Nero?

JOSEPHUS

Orestes.

Aliturus bangs his fist against his forehead.

ALITURUS

Now you've got me doing it!

But he doesn't want to go on being Emperor.

JOSEPHUS

So if he acts —

ALITURUS

What —

JOSEPHUS

At the end of the last act, he can come alive again.

On the stage, Nero goes to the centre and takes up the

position of an actor. Poppeia remains on the bench
holding the scroll.

Nero acts a scene from the *Oresteia*. When he speaks it is
as if he is playing two parts: the first line in a falsetto, and
the next in a bass.

> NERO

— I gave you life, let me grow old with you —

— What, kill my father, then you'd live with me? —

— Destiny had a hand in that, my child! —

— This too! Destiny is handing you your death! —

He stops acting.

> NERO

This is ridiculous!

> POPPEIA

I thought you were rather good.

> NERO

It's when you play all the parts yourself, it's ridiculous.

He goes to Poppeia and takes the scroll.

> POPPEIA

You can be both good and ridiculous —

> NERO

One man wrote it after all —

> POPPEIA

Like life —

> NERO

— Etcetera.

He glances into the camera.

Aliturus calls from the back of the gymnasium —

> ALITURUS

My lord —

Aliturus and Josephus come forward.

Nero points at Aliturus and acts —

> NERO

— You have no fear of a mother's curse my son? —

> JOSEPHUS

I think it's when one part of you is on good terms with
the other parts of you, when you are this part of you,
that of course all drama's ridiculous.

Nero looks at Josephus; then away; as if he had not heard him.

Poppeia smiles at Josephus. She murmurs —

POPPEIA

— Lose two turns —

NERO

Aliturus —

ALITURUS

Yes, my lord?

NERO

Have you found that fellow who came alive again?

POPPEIA

Does he smell?

NERO

Of course he doesn't smell!

POPPEIA

Well I would if I were him.

NERO

I thought you rather liked that sort of thing.

He faces Aliturus and acts —

NERO

— She must die, or she'll betray more men —

ALITURUS

I've found —

Poppeia murmurs —

POPPEIA

— And then can come alive again.

She glances into the camera.

ALITURUS

I've found one of his compatriots, my lord —

He gestures to Josephus.

Nero terms to Poppeia. He seems to quote —

NERO

— And we will sit on a bank where the wild thyme blows —

He goes to Poppeia and kisses her.

Then he faces Josephus and raises an arm. He acts —

57

NERO

— Art thou the Christ, the Son of God? —

— Art thou the King of the Jews? —

Josephus smiles.

Nero waits.

NERO

Oh yes, he didn't say anything, did he.

He lowers his arm.

POPPEIA

He said — You said it —

NERO

I said it?

POPPEIA

— You said it —

NERO

Oh God, a riddle —

I love riddles!

He speaks to Josephus —

NERO

Do you know the one about the Cretan who said —
All Cretans are liars —

JOSEPHUS

Yes. It isn't a matter of logic. It's a matter of time.

NERO

Of time?

JOSEPHUS

Yes. It takes time for you, or the Cretan, to say what you
say; and then to refer back to what you've said.

Nero looks put out.

NERO

I see. No I don't.

JOSEPHUS

Exactly. It isn't a contradiction. It's a narration. A
pulsation.

POPPEIA

A pulsation!

JOSEPHUS

A wave, a heartbeat.

Nero wanders away around the stage.

> NERO
>
> And the arrow that never reaches its target?
>
> ALITURUS
>
> You're dealing with what happens, and then the way you talk about what happens —
>
> NERO
>
> And the tortoise that is never caught by the hare?
>
> POPPEIA
>
> And the man who was dead and came alive?
>
> JOSEPHUS
>
> What has four legs in the morning, two in the after-noon, and three in the evening —
>
> NERO
>
> The Sphinx!
>
> POPPEIA
>
> No it isn't the Sphinx!
>
> NERO
>
> Oh it was the Sphinx who said it —

Nero stops and watches Josephus and Poppeia.
Josephus and Poppeia smile at each other.

> POPPEIA
>
> What is it then?
>
> JOSEPHUS
>
> In two of the images legs is a metaphor.
>
> POPPEIA
>
> And in the other?
>
> JOSEPHUS
>
> It is not.
>
> POPPEIA
>
> What is it then —
>
> JOSEPHUS
>
> When?
>
> POPPEIA
>
> This evening?

Poppeia begins to laugh.
Nero comes up to Josephus.

NERO

But if he didn't want to be king —

JOSEPHUS

Who: Oedipus? Christ? Nero?

NERO

He'd have to keep it secret —

JOSEPHUS

Or they'd kill him —

NERO

Exactly.

Nero walks round the stage again.

Josephus stays with Poppeia.

POPPEIA

Why are Jews circumcised, do you know?

JOSEPHUS

It's a sacrament.

POPPEIA

What's a sacrament?

JOSEPHUS

I'll tell you a story —

Nero comes up to Josephus.

NERO

You will keep it secret?

JOSEPHUS

It is.

NERO

What —

JOSEPHUS

By the nature of language.

Nero walks round the stage again.

Josephus speaks to Poppeia.

JOSEPHUS

— There were once two climbers on Mount Olympus. They were fastened to each other by rope. One fell, and was suspended from the other. This other had to cut either the rope or —

He looks at Poppeia.

After a time —

POPPEIA

Oh, the other thing!

Nero has come up.

NERO

Why?

POPPEIA

— Are Jews circumcised, do you know? —

Aliturus has moved away. He has gone over to a group of boys, who begin to undress him.

NERO

Either everyone dies, or one or two come alive again?

He watches Aliturus.

When the boys have undressed Aliturus, they lay him down on a bench and begin to whip him.

Poppeia speaks to Josephus. She does not seem to be acting.

POPPEIA

You will come and see us?

JOSEPHUS

Where will you be?

POPPEIA

In Greece, I think. They appreciate him in Greece.

JOSEPHUS

I thought this was Greece —

POPPEIA

No, dear, it's Rome.

Nero kicks at the pillars of the scenery.

NERO

Wood! Plastic!

He watches Aliturus.

NERO

Look at Aliturus, is he dying? Coming alive?

Josephus speaks as if quoting —

JOSEPHUS

— Just a little more modelling round the mouth, the eyes —

Nero turns to Josephus.

NERO

You don't think my mother will come alive again, do you?

JOSEPHUS

I thought you were playing all the parts.

NERO

But that was ridiculous.

Poppeia and Josephus continue to smile at one another.

POPPEIA

But if we know we're playing different parts —

Nero speaks to Josephus.

NERO

You think it'll work?

JOSEPHUS

What we're talking about is happening, isn't it?

VIII

Shortly before Lilia had gone with the man to the back of the aeroplane, Wolf Tanner, in the first-class compartment, put down Jason's typescript after he had read a few pages; held it on his knee; and said 'You're doing this as some sort of joke?'

Jason thought — Ah, you're a puritan!

Wolf Tanner said 'A review sketch? A satire? I mean, one of those things on television?'

Jason said 'It's true I'm making them out to be more intelligent than they probably were.'

He thought — I am making you out to be more intelligent than you probably are?

Wolf Tanner said 'Who?'

Jason said 'Nero. Poppeia.'

He thought — I could explain: Nero really was an actor; he really did care about aesthetics; he really did want to give up his boring life of being an emperor; there really was a rumour, after he had died, that he and Poppeia had become alive and well in Greece again —

— But still, no one might want to listen to this.

Lisa Grant had continued to make movements as if to get out of her chair. She had given up appearing to try to climb over the back: now she was having trouble with her seat-belt, magazines, handbag, dark glasses. Wolf Tanner's legs stretched like barricades across her way. She said 'Excuse me, darling.' Wolf Tanner said 'I didn't hear it, darling.' Lisa Grant stepped over his legs and pulled herself round into the seat across the aisle from Jason. She said 'Can I see your script?' Jason said 'Yes do.' Wolf Tanner put his hand with the script in it back over the top of his chair. Jason thought — He is like a photograph of a fast bowler in action.

He said 'It's a way of talking. It goes on in the mind — '

He thought — I am getting desperate.

He had been going to say — If one is to stay alive.

Lisa Grant took the script. She opened it. She stared at it as though she could not read. Then she said 'You think those people should not have killed themselves at Masada?'

Jason said 'I've not said that.'

'But you say — '

'I've said that as a symbol Masada's dangerous, if you care about a society's survival.'

'But do you?'

Lisa Grant was wearing a white blouse, a blue skirt, and no stockings. Jason thought — Her bones are as brittle as if suffering from fall-out.

He said 'Any society?'

She said 'Or that one.'

He thought — Would it be condescending to say that, yes, perhaps I do care more about a society of Jews?

He said 'I don't know what an individual should do if a society seems set on destroying itself. Perhaps it should be allowed to. I mean, perhaps it means a society should destroy itself so that what it stands for can go on.'

He thought — I do not have to explain, do I, that all life is paradoxical?

She said 'I'm a Jew.'

He thought — Then no, I don't have to explain this.

He said 'Jews seem to know so well the business of things having to be broken up in order that something shall live. But the thing is that now this is too dangerous. Something has to change, in the mind, if the world is to stay alive.'

Lisa Grant said 'And Jews can't do that?'

Jason said 'They've had enough practice at it.'

Lisa Grant said 'Then why don't they?'

Jason said 'I don't think they're at ease with it.'

Epstien called out from Jason's left — 'Hostess, can I have some more of that champagne?'

Jason thought — We are sitting on an H-bomb, with flints and powder.

Wolf Tanner was lying back with his eyes closed.

Lisa Grant said 'What would you be ready to die for?'

Jason said 'I suppose my family. My children.'

'But not your country?'

'That's never a proper question. My country is the country of my family, my children.'

She said 'You'd fight for it a certain amount — '

He thought — Well I did, didn't I?

She said ' — Until it seemed to want to destroy itself?'

He thought — Her arms are like branches stripped of bark. Then — Is there a child alive within the rubble?

He said 'It's a way of trying to see — '

She said 'And you'd just watch it — '

He said 'Well, one wouldn't be allowed to do just that.'

She said 'Why not?' Then — 'You'd be persecuted?'

He thought — She has had people in her family who have been persecuted?

He said 'That might make it easier to — '

'What — '

He thought — Dear God, no, one cannot be clever about that.

He had been about to say — Make it easier to bear?

He said 'At least one would not feel guilty.'

A hostess had come up with another bottle of champagne. She filled up Epstien's glass. Wolf Tanner held out his glass. Jason thought — We will all get drunk, to make things easier to bear?

Lisa Grant said 'You think Jews are cleverer than other people?'

He said 'They live out paradoxes — '

She said 'What paradoxes — '

He thought — She is not listening: I am repeating myself.

He said 'Things like getting schoolchildren to listen to Josephus at Masada.'

She said 'You think that is not loyal?'

He said 'Yes it is, if you know what you're doing.'

He thought — Then it would be this knowingness that would be scattered like seeds —

— But still this talk, however much repeated, would be taboo?

65

Epstien called out — 'And some champagne for my two friends here! My two friends at the back!'

Jason thought — Oh yes, who are those two at the back?

Then — Perhaps I can use them as a diversion, as I begin to destroy myself —

He said 'It's the responsibility that seems impossible.'

Lisa Grant said 'The responsibility for what?'

Jason said 'People like Jews might be running the world. But it's clever people who find it easier to complain.'

Lisa Grant said 'Does anyone run the world?'

Jason thought — That's the complaint?

Then — Perhaps it's just I who cannot bear my own voice continuing in the rubble.

Epstien called out — 'How are you two doing, all right?'

A man's voice from the back called — 'Fine!' Then a woman's — 'All right!'

Jason thought — That was a good voice.

Then — Rescue me!

He was leaning over the side of his seat facing Lisa Grant.

He began to say — 'I think the things they could have taken responsibility for — I mean taken responsibility in that they could have trusted them more — '

Epstien, behind him, suddenly shouted — 'I can't breathe!' He began to struggle with his seat-belt as if it were a snake wrapped round him.

Jason thought — He is like a child being strangled by his umbilical cord.

Lisa Grant said 'What?' Then — 'But how can things save you, that go on in the mind — '

Jason thought — A rope; a drainpipe; I can't remember.

Then — Children?

The steward came hurrying up to Epstien. He stretched over Jason to get at the air vent above Epstien's head. This blocked Jason's view of Lisa Grant.

Jason thought — The curtain has come down: perhaps we can now all leave the theatre.

It seemed there had been nothing, after all, with Lisa Grant, as with Epstien and Wolf Tanner, except reflections from liquids behind her eyes.

Then a voice beside him said 'Daddy!'

He said 'Hullo!'

He thought — Ah, that was what I had been going to say: what I have been looking for in the rubble: those bright eyes like angels!

He said 'What are you doing here?'

His child said 'Mummy's with that man.'

He said 'What man?'

His child said 'That man as has got sweeties in his bag.'

Jason thought — Well, after all, there is the question: what is a real battle and what is not?

The steward went away, having adjusted the nozzle above Epstien's head. Jason lifted his child on to his lap.

He said 'What is the man as has got sweeties in his bag?'

Then he leaned across to Lisa Grant and said 'The one thing they might have had more responsibility for, because they might have trusted them more, was children.'

Lisa Grant was looking past Jason at Epstien. Epstien was looking at the child.

Lisa Grant said 'Epstien, please stop interrupting our conversation.'

Epstien said 'Me interrupt your conversation?'

Jason thought he might say — You see it is children who are seeds, like messages —

Epstien said 'Where did that thing come from?'

Jason thought — Who get blown on the wind; who go between the unconscious and the conscious and not only in the mind —

His child looked between Jason and Epstien wonderingly.

Lisa Grant said 'Fuck off, Epstien.'

Epstien said 'Give her her commodores.'

Wolf Tanner said 'Not commodores with drinkies.'

Epstien said 'Hey Wolf, how's your partner?'

Wolf Tanner said 'Fuck off, Epstien.'

Lisa Grant said 'Don't talk like that about me!'

Epstien said 'Give her a brandy.'

Jason, holding his child, thought — Now what on earth is

happening? Epstien couldn't breathe? My child came in? There are horsemen pursuing us across a desert —

— And I had such a message to the world! about how being such messengers might save us —

He said 'But what's Mummy doing?'

His child was looking round at Epstien, then at Lisa Grant, then at Wolf Tanner.

Jason thought — But wouldn't it be an angel, in fact, that might blow up the world?

He thought he should get up and go to the tourist compartment —

— Going to and fro, like electricity?

His child said 'My want to fly the aeroplane!'

He said 'You can't fly the aeroplane.'

His child said 'My want to!'

The child looked for a moment as if he might cry; then he made a face like a comedian with the corners of his mouth turned down; then roared with laughter.

Jason thought — And I will have a chance to have a look at that woman, whoever she is, at the back on the right by the window.

He stood up. He took his child by the hand. He thought — Well, there was never much chance of my doing anything, was there, about the film, except make my own small explosion —

— But who is the man with sweeties?

He and his child went through the curtain at the back, past the steward's cabin, and into the tourist compartment. He thought — That girl is quite pretty, isn't she?

Beside her there had been a dark-haired man with spectacles. Jason had wondered — Don't I know him?

In the tourist compartment there were all the people packed as if in tombs waiting for the resurrection.

His child led him by the hand. He thought — We are like Virgil and Dante going into —

— Hell?

He could not see Lilia. He knew she would have tried to get a seat near the front, so that she would be one of the first to get food and whisky.

68

His child led him to three empty seats. On the two seats nearest to the window were the child's toys and Lilia's zip-bag. On the floor by the seat near the aisle was a bag out of which stuck the top of a bottle of whisky.

The child began climbing over the seats and collecting his orange juice and biscuits.

Jason thought — Well, what do I do now?

— It is as if we have got into some different time-warp.

He said 'Mummy's gone to pee?'

His child said 'Yes Mummy's gone to pee.'

He said 'How long have they been gone?'

His child climbed back and held him by the hand again.

There were an air hostess and an old woman like harpies watching him from the end of the aisle by the lavatories.

He thought — Dear God, what did Dante make of hell?

He said 'Well let's go back, shall we?'

His child looked up at him.

He thought — Well at least I might now chat with that pretty girl by the window.

The hostess, who was with the old woman, seemed about to come and speak to him.

He thought — But there are things one can't say?

He moved, with his child, back up the aisle to the first-class.

He thought — Why did I ever think I could defeat anybody?

Then — Hell is where it's better not even to ask what's going on.

He found that he did not even want to be with his child. He wanted to say — Go back and wait for Mummy.

Then he thought — But of course, they have gone to different lavatories!

Then — Why do I think these things about Lilia?

He held on to the hand of his child.

When he was back in the first-class compartment it was as if for a moment he did not recognize it. He said to himself — You go out through a door, along a corridor, in through the same door. Lisa Grant was now sitting by Epstien; the man with spectacles was standing in the aisle talking to the steward; Wolf Tanner was in the seat by the window on the right in front.

Jason thought — But it is I myself who am different: I have grown old, in the different time-warp.

— And I have given away the last two copies of my script: my children!

The man with spectacles, in the aisle, was looking at him curiously. Jason thought — He knows what's going on?

— In the lavatory?

— Or is it that I have some memory —

The man with spectacles said 'I can take him to fly the aeroplane if you like.'

Jason said 'What?'

The man with spectacles said 'I've asked the captain.' He held out his hand to the child.

Jason said 'That's extraordinarily kind!'

He thought — And the seat by the girl at the back will be free.

He said to the child 'You go with this kind man and fly the aeroplane.'

His child looked at him wonderingly.

Jason thought — But still, what on earth is happening?

His child went off with the man towards the captain's cabin. Jason turned to the seat at the back.

The girl said 'Come and sit here.'

He said 'Yes I will, thank you.'

The girl had a bright freckled face. He thought — She is Epstien's secretary? his mistress?

Then — She might be Scottish: and dance up and down between sword-blades.

The girl said 'He pulled her hair.'

He said 'Who pulled whose hair?'

He settled down. He noticed, which he had not done before, that Lisa Grant was crying.

He thought — Epstien pulled Lisa Grant's hair? Lisa Grant and Epstien are lovers?

Then — War has broken out everywhere.

He said 'You make it sound like *Pelléas et Mélisande*.'

The girl said 'Oh, did you have that in mind when you wrote about that courtyard?'

He thought — What courtyard?

Then he said 'You've been reading my script!'

The girl said 'Yes.'

He said 'How?' Then — 'You've got a copy?'

She said 'Yes.' Then — 'I know the girl who typed it.'

Jason thought — You see, there are these connections that come to help you —

Then — Oh well, here we go, O Lilia.

IX

Lilia, in the tourist-class compartment, held Jason's typescript on her knee. She closed her eyes. She was remembering —

— We had been at a dinner party, Jason and I, and he had been talking, talking: oh God, how he sometimes talks! his face taking on the daemonic look of a gargoyle or a satyr; spouting out rain from the roofs of his cathedrals; scattering it over the heads of the other people at the table; saying —

— You think the miseries of the world are caused by political systems? What political system has ever made much difference to the sum of human miseries! Human beings need miseries like snails need shells: to get out of the heat of the sun; to sit in a cave watching cinema screens showing miseries; and so they get pleasure. There was that tower people were supposed to be building to heaven; then they had to get back home to watch miseries on television. Home is where you watch other people squashed together in a box; treading on each other's faces: these images are in the mind: you know where you are with them. If anyone wants to be out in the sun, out of the cave, they have to be alone. This is what is godlike: what people were building to heaven. But then you go mad. Or you have to pretend to be mad to protect yourself. So what's the difference. Who wants to be godlike in public except a few mad archaic statues on the road to Rome or Moscow or somewhere; smiling and watching the faces of the defeated going the other way. Human beings should be aesthetic, but they are not, they think they are moral. But they can't face being morally superior to gods.

And she had thought — How often have I heard this! these paradoxes spewed out over people's heads as if from the gargoyles of cathedrals: you say there are some things that cannot be said: for God's sake don't say them.

Then in the car going home she had said to him 'You just want to shock people who aren't as clever as yourself.'

He said 'You mean I demean myself?'

She said 'Yes.'

He said 'If I demean myself, then I'm showing people they're as clever as myself.'

They were driving through a poor part of London where on Saturday night people had been turned out of pubs and were standing around on street corners. It was an area where immigrants had gathered, and in the half-dark of lamplight people gave the impression of being in fancy dress or wearing masks. Like a Venetian painting, she thought, with people assembled for some nefarious joke or crime. She wondered — Black people are so much older and more sophisticated than ourselves! She said to Jason 'But you only pretend to demean yourself like a dreadful condescending god coming down.' He said 'What else is condescending except coming down?' She thought — I can't bear this: you protect yourself with your cleverness so far back that it's as if you were in a womb. She shouted 'Stop the car!' She thought — I must get away from this monster child. Jason drove on steadily; then he accelerated as if he were going to drive into a brick wall. She thought — Oh I know, I know, you will now pretend to kill us just to prove you have feelings! Then he put the brakes on violently. She said 'I want to get out.' He said 'All right get out.' She thought — It's cold, I'm a long way from home, this is a part of town where women are dragged off to basements and raped and murdered or something. Then — Or is it because of social conditioning that I imagine this? Jason leaned across and opened the car door for her. She got out. She thought — All I said was that I wanted to get out! She moved off up the road. She thought — If he comes after me I can pretend to be being dragged off to a basement and raped or murdered or something: then he will feel sorry. But what if he does not come after me? Is this how we demean ourselves? Jason did not seem to be coming after her. She thought — This is, in fact, quite likely how one gets raped. It was such a quiet part of town, with men not even standing on street corners. She seemed to have walked an enormous distance. Then she heard a car coming up behind her. She thought — I can fling my arms out like people do in films; in an alleyway with a car behind them and nowhere to escape to and then he will run over me, and I can lie there and pretend to be dead, till he is sorry, and then I can come alive again like one of Shakespeare's heroines. The car went past. She thought — Dear God, he will not really drive home, will he, and leave me to be raped and murdered in this part of town? The car drew up about twenty yards past her. She thought — But I do see the impossible position I have put him in: if he drives home he'll feel guilty, and if he waits he'll be giving in: he can't win. Jason got out of the car. She wondered — So what will he do about it? He had left the door to the driving seat open. He began walking off in front of her up the road. He called back — 'You take the car!' She thought — But it is now I who am in an impossible position! I will either feel guilty, or I will have to give in: I can't win.

She looked into the car. He had left the keys in the ignition switch.

She thought — I suppose I could leave the car and we could both walk home: but I need the car in the morning.

— Or I could drive about twenty yards past him and then pull up and get out and we could play this game of leapfrog all the way home —

— like this little piggy went to market.

She got into the car. She started it. She thought — Well, in fact, no one wins: but it's you who think you're good at getting out of this sort of treadmill, isn't it, O Jason.

She drove slowly up the street in the direction in which he had gone. She peered from side to side. She seemed to have lost him.

She thought — Dear God, he's not going to pretend he's being raped or murdered in a basement, is he? —

— Because, hard luck, things like that just don't happen to men.

Then suddenly he appeared in the headlights in front of her. He had stepped into the middle of the road and he flung his arms out. She thought — Oh no, he's not doing that thing of being trapped in an alleyway with a car coming up behind him is he? I thought of that first, how boring. There was in fact a high wall along one side of the road beyond which was probably a railway. Then Lilia saw in front of Jason a group of men, or boys, on a street corner: they were facing him. She thought — Dear God, are they really going to drag him down to a basement and beat him up and murder him or something? Things like that do happen to men, don't they? In her sudden anxiety she put her feet down on what seemed to be all three pedals on the floor at once: the car shot forwards; then halted; then seemed to heave up and down like an elephant being sick. She thought — This is ridiculous. Then she switched off the ignition: she could think of nothing else to do. The car backfired loudly. Jason began to stagger across the road as if he had been shot. He held his stomach. She thought — Oh do stop acting! Then — That's that film about Dublin in the late 1940s, isn't it? That was quite a good film. Then — But has he really been shot? Jason had reached the side of the road; he put a hand out against the wall; he sank slowly on to his knees. She thought — What was that film called? The group of men and boys on the street corner had been watching him; then, as she opened the car door, they turned and ran. She thought — Well, this is one way of getting rid of them. She went over to Jason. He was lying on the ground with his cheek pressed against the wall. She thought — Well how better could we have managed this? She said 'Oh do get up!' Jason said 'Act five scene three.' She said 'What is act five scene three?' He said 'When they're all dead, and then come alive again.' She thought — How many times have I heard that! But what I see is, yes, how else could we have got rid of all this ridiculous quarrelling in our unconscious? Jason had been holding his hand against his heart inside his coat; he now took it out and stared at it as if there were blood on it. He said 'Where is it?' She said 'Where is what?' He said 'My wallet!' She said 'Oh do come on, I want to go to bed.' He said 'Well I'm afraid I can't, dearie, unless you'll do it for free.' Then he began to laugh. He laughed so much he rolled over in the gutter. She said 'Oh yes, yes, you're quite funny.' She thought — Well he is, isn't he?

Then, when he had got up briskly and taken out his wallet

and looked at it and they were driving home in the car again he said 'Do you think one could in fact disperse crowd scenes like that?'

She said 'No.'

She thought — You do really think people on street corners are there for your benefit, don't you.

Then in the middle of the night when she had been asleep for some time — she had been thinking: Yes, yes, this is all very well, but are we not still trying to be too much like gods —

In the middle of the night she woke because she heard him groan beside her. She put out a hand and felt his hands pressed against his face. She said 'What is it? What is it?'

He said 'I feel so horrible!'

She said 'Why?'

He said 'So horrible! So horrible!'

She thought — Is there not some line in a book like this?

She said 'It's all right!'

He said 'Everything you say is true!'

She thought — It is the middle of the night: and I have so much to do in the morning.

She said 'What do I say?'

He said 'That I'm contemptuous, arrogant. That I don't care about other people. This thing I'm writing — how can people live like that!'

She thought — This'll teach me to say things like that!

She said 'What thing you're writing?'

He said 'About Josephus. This play-acting. This trying to be like gods. Of course human beings are flesh and blood! To pretend to be like gods is loathsome.'

She thought — But people have to try, don't they?

Then — I've got to go and look at a school for the child in the morning.

He said 'Flesh and blood are to do with pain.'

She said 'Well you're in pain.'

He said 'Of course loyalty matters!'

She said 'But you're saying all this.'

He said 'What am I saying?'

She said 'That loyalty matters. That when something else

76

matters it's sometimes frightening, as in your script.'

She thought — And sometimes you need me to play all this back to you before morning.

He said 'Go on — '

She thought — Can't we go to sleep now?

She said 'You'll know all this in the morning!'

She was about to go to sleep again — she had some vision of her child running across a desert with a shadow chasing it as if from an aeroplane — when Jason said —

'Of course you have to fight for a better society. Or how can the world get any better?'

She thought — And all this because I said in the car —

— But what was that shadow coming after the child like a bird, a helicopter?

Jason said 'You know that story about when I was nearly taken prisoner in that war — '

She thought — Do I know that story of when you were nearly taken prisoner in that war! —

He said 'I was in the army, you know, because I had to be, I was still quite young. It was after the real war, we were in Cyprus, there was still that sort of war. I wanted to do what I had to do, but I did not want to die. What was the point of dying, it was a useless war. We were just holding on, while politicians quarrelled. You see, I was quite like Josephus. I was doing a job, in the hills; then some of us were taken prisoner. I mean, there wasn't much I could do; it had been my turn to sleep; our men didn't fire a shot. They didn't want to die: they knew it was a useless war: they weren't like the men with Josephus. But then when we were being taken away — the people who'd captured us said they wouldn't hurt us: they just wanted us as hostages for some sort of bargaining — when we were being taken away I felt — I don't know — But I can't be taken prisoner! I had to get away, even if it meant they shot me. Which they might have done. It was the one way they might have done, in the mix-up. But there was all this damn dead rubbish like pride, you see, and honour. Without which what is life worth living for. So I did get away. And they could have shot me. In fact someone nearly did. One of our own people. But I

77

got away. I couldn't, when it came to it, be like Josephus!'

When she put her hand out to him again she found he was shaking. She held him. She said 'It's all right! It's all right.'

He said 'That damned dead rubbish!'

She said 'But it was for yourself — '

He said 'What was?'

She said 'Your pride: your honour.'

After a time he said 'In a different context?'

She thought — Come on, you're supposed to be clever.

She said 'You wanted to be alive, didn't you?'

He said 'You mean, like Josephus?'

Then — 'You are clever!'

Then he rolled over and made love to her.

Afterwards, he said 'Do you know how I got away?'

She thought — Do I, in fact, know how he got away?

He said 'There was this man who took a shot at me. One of our reinforcements coming up. He didn't know who I was. He thought I was one of them. So I lay with my head against a wall and pretended to be dead, till he went away.

She thought — I love you so much: please can I go to sleep now?

He said 'Poor bloody humans! poor bloody sods!'

She said 'Of course, it's what you make of things.'

She thought — Now why did I say that?

Then — I'm sleeping?

Just before she had gone to sleep, or had woken, there had been the sound of an aeroplane coming in — her child running across a desert —

Jason had been saying 'You've given me a new scene to write!'

She had thought — There you are then!

She was in the tourist-class compartment of an aeroplane. She was waking. She thought — But now what time am I in? That scene was not the one —   What is happening?

Then — There was that picture of Mary and Joseph and the infant Jesus crossing the desert on their donkey.

X

SCENE: Jerusalem, 66 A.D. A courtyard, with a loggia and a fountain.

Josephus is lying on a couch. He is covered with rugs as if he were ill.

Queen Berenice, a woman in her thirties, wearing sackcloth and with her head shorn, is walking up and down. It is as if she were rehearsing a speech.

From outside there comes occasionally the roar of a crowd.

BERENICE

— Fight the Romans and you'll be defeated. Be defeated, and you'll be scattered and spread what you believe in throughout the world. So, if you want to spread your beliefs, fight and be defeated —

She turns to Josephus.

BERENICE

I can't say that.

JOSEPHUS

Why not?

BERENICE

Anyway, they wouldn't believe me.

JOSEPHUS

Then that's all right.

BERENICE

Why?

JOSEPHUS

Then they'll fight, and be defeated.

Berenice walks up and down.

She seems to rehearse her speech —

BERENICE

— Fight, and you'll be doing as the Romans do. So why

fight them if you want to be like the Romans? —
She breaks off.

BERENICE

It goes round and round.

JOSEPHUS

— But if you're defeated, then what you'll spread will
be about defeat —

BERENICE

And we want to win —

JOSEPHUS

Don't we.

Berenice watches Josephus.

BERENICE

So — Don't fight? Don't win?

Josephus lies with his eyes closed.

BERENICE

A riddle.
— I like riddles —
Who said that?

JOSEPHUS

The Emperor.

BERENICE

I wish you'd introduce me.

JOSEPHUS

Perhaps I will.

BERENICE

When he's dead?

Josephus sits up and coughs and bangs his chest.

JOSEPHUS

You can't say that!

BERENICE

A joke! I didn't mean it!

Josephus lies back.
The crowd roars outside.
Berenice turns in the direction of the crowd.

BERENICE

— My friends, you must both be defeated and not be
defeated in order to spread God's word. So, seven-

thirty this evening, come to the Coliseum! —
She turns to Josephus.

BERENICE

That'll kill them.

JOSEPHUS

You can't say it: you can say it if you say you can't say
it —

BERENICE

— You'll be the death of me —
Josephus sits up.

JOSEPHUS

You know what a riddle is?
A sieve —
He sings —

JOSEPHUS

— She went to sea in a sieve she did —
— In a sieve she went to sea —
Then he speaks in his ordinary voice —

JOSEPHUS

But there were quite a few of them left in Rome.
After the waters had run over them.
He lies back.

BERENICE

Who?
Oh yes I see.
You have to keep it moving —
You have to keep it secret.
She turns in the direction of the crowd again.

BERENICE

— My friends, if you want to win, don't know what
you're doing, because if you do, you couldn't do it.
But if you know this is what you're doing, then —
She breaks off.
She turns to Josephus.

BERENICE

You stay alive?

JOSEPHUS

Win —

BERENICE
But can't say —
JOSEPHUS
It's called the indeterminacy principle.
A higher logical type.
BERENICE
What dreadful phrases!
JOSEPHUS
Yes aren't they.
You can't know and say at the same time.
What you say alters what is known —
So when you know this —
Josephus sits up and arranges his rugs.
BERENICE
Like the Cretan —
JOSEPHUS
Yes like the Cretan.
Or wasn't he a Galilean?
The crowd roars outside.
BERENICE
And in the meantime —
JOSEPHUS
Give them what they want.
He lies back and closes his eyes.
Berenice turns in the direction of the crowd. She acts —
BERENICE
— Oh children, children! You have a city and a home! —
— And when we have parted, there you will stay for
ever! —
— You motherless; I miserable —
She breaks off.
BERENICE
I used to play that. Medea.
JOSEPHUS
I think a little more nobility round the mouth, the eyes —
BERENICE
She's about to kill her children —
To hurt their father.

JOSEPHUS

Yes, everyone likes that.

I suppose everyone at some time wants to kill their children. And hurt their loved one.

The crowd roars outside.

Berenice turns in the direction of the crowd. She acts —

BERENICE

— I cannot do it! I will take them! —

— Why should I hurt them to make their father suffer! —

JOSEPHUS

Because you think that if you do you won't suffer. But of course, you will.

BERENICE

Who?

JOSEPHUS

Medea. Jason.

Berenice watches him.

BERENICE

You go in and out of context —

JOSEPHUS

Who?

BERENICE

You.

JOSEPHUS

But still suffer.

BERENICE

Do you?

JOSEPHUS

You're the same person. Aren't you?

He smiles.

Berenice watches him.

Then she turns and acts —

BERENICE

— I must steel myself to it! What a coward I am! —

— Tempting my resolution with soft talk! —

She breaks off.

BERENICE

And then?

JOSEPHUS

A child's scream is heard from inside the house —

BERENICE

In the mind —

JOSEPHUS

In the play —

BERENICE

And in fact?

JOSEPHUS

What are you going to do with those children?

Berenice watches him.

Josephus lies with his eyes closed.

BERENICE

That's why you're ill?

Josephus sits up and coughs and bangs his chest.

BERENICE

A joke! Sorry!

She walks up and down again.

BERENICE

— You look like death warmed up —

JOSEPHUS

If you can stop breathing, you can stay alive for three days.

BERENICE

And if you can't?

JOSEPHUS

Go in and out of context. Come alive. Look at what you say.

BERENICE

A higher logical type —

JOSEPHUS

Look after the children.

He settles back in his chair again.

Berenice watches him.

BERENICE

And in the meantime —

84

There comes into the courtyard Philomela, a girl of seventeen. She goes to the fountain to get water.

Josephus sits up and acts —

JOSEPHUS
— Is she one of us? —

Berenice acts —

BERENICE
— I promised never to say! —

JOSEPHUS
— Then never do! —

Then he leans forward and speaks to Philomela as if in code —

JOSEPHUS
— Hullo —

PHILOMELA
— Hullo —

JOSEPHUS
— I wondered if you remembered me —

PHILOMELA
— Oh yes, I loved only you, you see —

JOSEPHUS
— I've never loved anyone else in my life —

BERENICE
You two know each other?

JOSEPHUS
Now why do you say that?

He lies back.

Philomela goes out, carrying water.

BERENICE
I see. No I don't see.
What's left? At the end?
In the sieve? The riddle?

JOSEPHUS
It's called —

BERENICE
I don't care what it's called!

JOSEPHUS
— Affirming the consequent —

— Survival of the fittest —

BERENICE

What dreadful phrases!

JOSEPHUS

Yes aren't they.

He lies with his eyes closed.

Berenice walks round the courtyard.

After a time Josephus calls out to her as if he were a prompter —

JOSEPHUS

— I say, when are you going to Rome? —

BERENICE

It's the connections?

But you must have something to contain them?

JOSEPHUS

— You can learn one or two things there you know! —

BERENICE

A stage? An audience?

She looks into the camera.

Philomela comes in again carrying a scroll. She hands this to Josephus.

Josephus sits up to read it.

After a time —

BERENICE

What does it say?

JOSEPHUS

War has been declared!

He tries to stand. He staggers. He puts a hand on his heart.

JOSEPHUS

I have been appointed commander of the Jewish forces in Galilee!

BERENICE

What does it really say?

Josephus acts solemnly —

JOSEPHUS

— Except a corn of wheat fall into the ground and die it abideth alone —

He hands the scroll back to Philomela.

BERENICE

But you do abide alone —

JOSEPHUS

So I don't die. Exactly.

He puts an arm round Philomela.
Berenice watches them.

BERENICE

You two do know each other!

Josephus acts —

JOSEPHUS

— Well, someone's got to go! I mean, one can't go on
letting them get away with it, can one; that dreadful
show at the Colosseum —

BERENICE

You mean, you're really —

JOSEPHUS

But don't be taken in by —

He holds Philomela at arm's length and looks at her.

JOSEPHUS

— My breastplate of righteousness! My armour of
light! —

He kisses her.

JOSEPHUS

Meet me behind the proscenium. Twenty minutes.

Philomela goes out.

BERENICE

But you may be killed —

JOSEPHUS

And come alive —

BERENICE

You'll betray them?

JOSEPHUS

Aren't all the best disciples betraying their loved ones
this season? —

He goes and puts an arm round Berenice. He kisses her.

JOSEPHUS

Meet me behind the gasworks. Thirty minutes.

Philomela returns carrying a breastplate. Josephus turns

it this way and that. He tries it on.

Berenice watches him.

Then she acts dramatically —

BERENICE

— Ah what a death hath found thee, little one! —

JOSEPHUS

All right, all right!

BERENICE

Hecuba.

She was always mourning children.

PHILOMELA

The children will be hidden.

BERENICE

Where?

PHILOMELA

At Masada.

Berenice and Josephus act as if they had not heard her.

BERENICE

It's a way of dealing with it? Of staying alive?

JOSEPHUS

Actually, I think I'll make quite a good soldier.

Berenice seems to alternate between acting and not acting —

BERENICE

— You may be tortured —

JOSEPHUS

I don't think one can say much more than —

BERENICE

You make me mad!

JOSEPHUS

You're not pregnant, are you?

BERENICE

— My higher logical type!

XI

In the first-class compartment Jason, seated next to the girl at the back, flipped through the pages of the typescript she had taken out of her bag, and said 'Why did you think that courtyard was to do with *Pelléas et Mélisande?*'

The girl said 'Oh well, your script's to do with all those sorts of connections, isn't it?'

He thought — You are my Philomela? My Berenice?

Then — But what is Lilia to the man as has got sweeties in his bag?

He said 'What's your name?'

She said 'Jane.' Then — 'I'm afraid so.'

He thought — So in this cold world in which people like particles wander and bump into and destroy each other there are still some which might go on, aren't there, having created particles of light —

He said 'I suppose it's by connections we make things — '

She said 'But how dò they help us to stay alive?'

Looking at her he thought — With your grey-green eyes and a tongue like water —

He said 'Well, if the world's like that — '

She said 'Stuff — '

He said 'Yes.'

He thought — You mean stuff of the universe, or the other stuffing —

She said 'Don't look at me like that!'

He thought he might put his hand on his heart and say — How should I look at you?

He said 'Why did Epstien pull Lisa Grant's hair? I mean, what goes on between those three in Rome?'

Jane said 'Well I suppose Epstien's in love with Wolf, and Wolf's trying to make it somehow with Lisa, and Lisa's got this little girl sort of thing with Epstien.'

'And they all travel round together.'

'And they all travel round together.'

'Like that play about hell.'

'Yes like that play about hell.'

Jason thought — Those grey-green eyes have something spilled over them like penicillin.

Jane said 'There was a terrible scene in the hotel. Wolf tried to bite off Epstien's cock.'

Jason thought — There's a fairy-story, isn't there, about a Wolf, or Peter, or someone, swallowing a cock?

Jane said 'They had to send for a doctor.'

Jason said 'And what happened then?'

Jane said 'Wolf said — I think I've bitten off even less than I can chew.' She began to laugh.

Jason thought — Yes, it does help if you are witty.

He said 'And what was Lisa doing?'

Jane said 'Oh Lisa was alight.'

Jason thought — Alight? Does that mean drunk? On drugs? She set fire to herself in the hotel lobby?

He said 'What is alight.'

Jane said 'Oh, heroin.'

She was staring at Jason with her bright, belligerent eyes.

Jason thought — Should I appear to be dazed? as if I were on drugs?

He said 'And what were you doing?'

Jane said ' — What was a nice girl like me doing — ?'

Jason said 'Yes.'

She said 'I like watching it.' Then — 'Didn't Josephus like watching it?'

He thought — I don't know: did he?

Then — I am in danger of moralising.

— Like that night when I got out of the car with Lilia —

He said 'But Josephus wasn't part of it.'

She said 'Oh I'm not part of it!'

He thought — They all say that.

He said 'You're Epstien's secretary or something?'

She said 'Yes I'm Epstien's secretary or something.'

He thought suddenly — If I don't moralise, of course she wants to get out!

He said 'And who is this Wolf's partner, that they talk about?'

She seemed suddenly unaccountably embarrassed.

He thought — But for her to get out, still, someone will have to suffer —

— It will not be her?

She said 'Oh, he's someone called Julius.'

'Julius — '

'He's someone they picked up in Rome. They wanted to leave him behind, but — '

Jason had been going to say — He's not on the plane?

Then he thought — Here, I will suffer?

She said 'Oh I know it's very childish: very silly — '

He thought — He's not the man as has got sweeties in his bag?

She said ' — But what isn't. Life's a fuck-up.'

He thought — Perhaps I could take you to a hotel by the Red Sea and we could hold hands and run along the beach together —

She said 'You don't think life's a fuck-up?'

He said 'No.'

He thought — I won't be moralising if I'm in pain?

She said 'Why not?'

He said 'Life's aesthetic.'

She said 'You believe in God?'

He said 'God's a word for the way things happen.'

'Which is — '

'Aesthetic.'

'How.'

'Things make patterns.'

'We make patterns — '

'Yes, but we couldn't if they weren't there.'

'What — '

'I've said this.'

'Connections — '

He thought — I think I can fight this, do I, if Lilia is with that man as has got sweeties?

Jane said ' — And such and such dies, and such and such stays alive — '

He said 'It's the sometimes wanting other people to die that's difficult.'

He thought — She knows I knew she was embarrassed?

Then — But is it not they who want to die, those clever people from Rome?

She said 'But the Christians founded a church.'

He thought — Dear God, it's not myself who wants to go on these journeys across deserts —

He said 'They founded a church on the man who denied Christ.'

'That's important?'

'I think so.'

'Why?'

'Then you can see what the choice is.'

'What — '

'You have to have something to hold it: to keep it alive.'

'The choice — '

'Yes.'

'But what holds it betrays it — '

'But is not itself the choice.'

He looked round again as if for some means of escape. He thought — I think it is I who suffer, in my town like Jotapata?

Jane said 'The choice is — '

He said 'Between knowing there is a choice or not.'

She said 'But not being chosen — '

He said 'I suppose it depends when you begin.'

He remembered — Upon everything we have ever been, to ourselves and to each other —

He wanted to cry out — Where are you, O Lilia?

Jane said 'They're all such characters.'

He said 'Who?' Then — 'Epstien and Wolf Tanner and Lisa Grant?'

He wanted to say — Characters are the parts of you that have died or should die —

— Like that man as has got sweeties?

He saw his child coming back down the aisle from the

cockpit of the aeroplane. He thought — But that is what we have ever been, O Lilia, to ourselves and to each other!

His child was being followed by the man with spectacles. Jason thought — There is that shadow on the wall that I think I know —

His child said 'Daddy — '

He said 'Yes?'

'My fly the aeroplane!'

Jason lifted the child on to his knee. He said 'How did you fly the aeroplane?'

His child said 'The aeroplane not coming down!'

Jason thought — Ah, my darling, like that first bird that flew out of the ark —

The man with spectacles had stopped in the aisle. He was talking to Epstien and Lisa Grant; but he was looking at Jason.

Jason said to Jane 'Who is that man?'

Jane said 'He's called Spud.'

Jason said 'I think I know him.'

Jane said 'He's the production manager.' Then — 'How do you know — '

Jason said 'Know that man?'

Jane said 'Know that God's aesthetic.'

He thought — Well, shall I say: it's when what you're thinking or talking about is happening at the same time —

The man called Spud said looking at Jason 'They're having a bit of trouble at Tel Aviv airport.'

Jason thought — There is too much going on: like lights coming on in a theatre.

After a time Wolf Tanner said 'Oh, what sort of trouble?'

Spud said 'They don't know yet. The captain said I could tell you people, but he doesn't want it known yet in the tourist-class.'

Jason thought — I have some memory of war?

He said to Jane 'You see it. Trust it.'

Jane said 'What?'

One of the hostesses was leaning over Lisa Grant. She was holding out a glass to her and saying 'Drink this.'

Jason thought — Perhaps Lisa Grant will grow bigger and

93

bigger and will burst out of the side of the plane like Alice in
Wonderland; or like that man in that film, what was its name —

— Or myself getting away in that war?

He said to Jane 'It's when so many things start happening at
the same time — '

Then he thought — But of course I know that man!

Jane said again 'What — '

Jason said 'Who are you?'

The man called Spud said 'Spud.'

Jason said 'I knew you in that war!'

Spud said 'Yes.'

Jane said 'It's what keeps you alive?'

Spud said 'I thought I'd shot you.'

Jason said to Jane 'What?' Then to the man — 'Yes.' Then —
'You were sitting behind a tank.'

Spud said 'I thought you were one of them.'

Jason said to Jane 'I was getting away.'

Jane said 'And now you're one of us.' She put her head against
his shoulder and laughed.

He thought — But now, with my child on my knee —

Then Jane sat back and said 'Look, I must tell you — '

He said 'Tell me what?'

He thought — One goes backwards and forwards; in place
and time; in imagination —

Jane said 'They had a plot, in Rome — '

The man called Spud had turned away.

Jason thought — Will I now be like Josephus, putting on my
breastplate?

She said 'You know how they always like breaking up happy
marriages — '

He said 'Yes.'

When he looked at her he thought — She has not been
laughing: she is crying?

Then — With that white light coming down: the curtain still
up in the theatre —

She said 'Well, they had this sort of plot, this bet, with this
man called Julius.'

Jason held his child on his knee. He thought — How cold it is!

Then — Ah well, it makes it more simple, doesn't it, when war is officially declared?

Epstien was saying 'We'll have to be diverted?'

Spud was saying 'We don't know that yet.'

Jason thought — A Bomb might have gone off?

He said to Jane 'What bet?'

He thought — That's why —

Jane said 'It was really Epstien's plot. He'd heard that you'd married. I suppose he's jealous of you. And your new wife. But also of Wolf and Julius. Wolf was angry.'

She did not say anything more.

Jason thought — Yes, you see, there are things you can't say. — Including, that I may kill someone.

He said 'This man called Julius is travelling in the tourist-class?'

Jane said 'Yes.' Then — 'I thought I'd better tell you.'

Jason said 'Right.' He thought — But what do you think you have told me?

Wolf Tanner was saying 'Where might we be diverted to?'

Jason thought — Ladies and gentlemen, there is a bomb: will everyone who wishes leave the theatre.

Jason's child said 'My want to see Mummy.'

Jason thought — But the man might be dangerous?

Then — But is not everything, and the child part of it, dangerous in this cold world?

Jane said 'You see why I think life's a fuck-up.'

He said 'Then why not change it.'

He had a vision, suddenly, of a man coming through the door of the first-class compartment with a gun and saying — This is a hijack. Jason would swivel in his seat and kick his hand and the gun would go off and there would be a small hole in the side of the plane which would grow bigger and bigger till they were all sucked towards it as if it were a black hole at the end of space and they would be like that man in that film, what was its name —

He said to his child 'Yes, go and find Mummy.'

Jane said 'I'm so sorry.'

He said 'About what?'

Spud, in the aisle, was saying 'No need to panic. We'll come down somewhere.'

Wolf Tanner was saying 'What goes up must come down.'

Lisa Grant was saying 'Speak for yourself, darling.'

Epstien was lying on his back like a turtle.

Jason thought — If Epstien is the God that is dead —

Spud remained in the aisle with his arms on the backs of two seats smiling down at Jason.

Jason thought — And this man called Spud is his pope, his production manager —

Jane said 'You still don't think life's a fuck-up?'

Jason said to his child 'Go and tell Mummy that the aeroplane's not coming down, and I'm with the man who thought he'd shot me in that war but hadn't.'

XII

When Lilia woke in the body of the aeroplane she did not know how long she had been asleep; she had had a vision of her child running across a desert landscape with the shadow of an aeroplane coming after; she had gone back in her memory to the night when Jason had got out of the car and then had told her about how he had escaped in the war; then she had gone into dream. She thought — We make these journeys in our minds, to oases, across a desert. She had the impression that the man beside her had at one time got up to go again to the back of the plane. Now from the seat beside her there came noises of eating. She thought — Or he is that dark horseman, shadow, pursuing us across a desert? Then — The journey across the desert was made by Mary, and Joseph, and the infant Jesus.

She found that she had a tray in front of her. It had been placed there, like some sort of man-trap, while she had been asleep.

She said 'I must go and look for my child!'

The man beside her said 'You're going to tell?'

She said 'Tell who what?'

She stirred. She remembered — Oh yes, this man is like one of Herod's horsemen with a desperate thing about sex.

He said 'Tell your husband — '

She said 'You're not going on about that.'

He said 'You liked it.'

She said 'I quite liked it.'

He said 'You want to do it again?'

On the tray in front of her was tinned salmon, salad, and chicken. She thought — And Jason will have had caviare and quails.

Then — This man could in fact be dangerous?

She began to eat.

The man said 'He didn't even buy you a first-class ticket!'

She said 'Who?'

He said 'Your husband.'

She thought — But what on earth can the man do? I will say he is mad: that he asked me to give him an injection.

She said 'Well, your boyfriend didn't buy you a first-class ticket.'

He said 'You know him?'

She said 'No of course not.'

The man began smiling and rubbing his hands along his thighs. He said 'He's my partner.'

She thought — What an extraordinarily boring bit of information.

Then — But if this man is ill, or on drugs, it won't be so difficult to deal with him —

— Doesn't he see that?

While she was eating, she tried to hold Jason's typescript on her knee. She thought — What would you have to say, O Jason, to this man who is after us —

— Would you say it is because I am the one who was abused, that I feel I have power?

She read —

Jerusalem, 66 A.D. The crowd outside the palace.
A man is making an inaudible speech: the crowd are chanting unintelligible slogans.
A Zealot in a white robe moves through the crowd. He has fair wavy hair and a painted face. He comes up behind a tall man in a toga. He pulls out a knife and stabs the man with no attempt at concealment. The tall man falls. The Zealot puts the knife under his cloak. Then he begins wailing, as if lamenting the death of the tall man. Some of the crowd turn to watch. Then the Zealot stops, bows, and goes off through the crowd as if at the end of a performance.

Lilia thought — Well, what does that mean, O Jason?
— You are the bearded man? This other man is the Zealot?

— He is also an actor?

The man beside her said 'I could tell him.'

She said again 'Tell who what?'

He said 'My partner.'

She thought — Your partner is on the plane?

Then — I must be careful here.

She said 'I'd say you were lying.'

'You'd tell a lie?'

'Of course I would.'

He said 'Well I wouldn't.'

She thought — Oh you know what truth is, do you?

She went back to Jason's typescript.

> The Zealot, in his white robe, enters a riding-school or gymnasium. In it there are people holding a goat. They are trying to drag it to an altar, on which there is a phallus. The Zealot gets down on all fours, with his back to the goat.

Lilia thought — Good heavens, I am the Zealot? I am the goat?

Then — But with this sort of game, one can make what one wants of anything, like throwing those sticks —

Then — But is this, or is it not, how one finds out truth, O Jason?

The man beside her said 'Look — '

She said 'Yes?'

He said 'Each one of these can kill you.'

He was holding out on the palm of his hand a box containing what seemed to be small white pills. He poked at them delicately with a finger.

He said 'They were carried by the Nazi leaders at the time of the Second World War.'

She thought — Oh yes, does not Jason say, those people were always trying to get themselves killed —

The man said 'And they're what are issued to the East German security forces now.'

She thought — Well there can't be any more boring bit of

99

information than that.

She tried to go back to her reading.

She thought — But our child is all right with you, isn't he, O Jason?

A room in another part of the town.

A man is counting gold coins from a bag. He hears footsteps: he looks for somewhere to hide the coins. He swallows them.

Zealots in white robes burst in. They ransack the furniture, slash the cushions. Then they notice that the man is looking ill.

They put their ears to his stomach. They get their knives ready.

This scene should be played as comedy.

Lilia thought — Good heavens!

Then — You mean, you could do it as a ballet?

— A ballet is a way of showing what's true?

The man beside her said 'I've got a tooth.'

She said 'You've got a tooth.'

The man had opened his mouth and was pointing inside.

He said 'Hollowed out. And with one of these inside.'

She said 'One of what?'

He pointed to the pills.

She said 'That must be useful.'

She tried to go back to her reading.

He said 'Then if I bite on it — '

She thought — If I'd bitten on your cock —

She looked up. She thought — Any obsession, any boringness, is a wanting to die.

Then — He is on cocaine? heroin?

She said 'Is it your own tooth?'

He said 'What do you mean, is it my own tooth?'

She said 'I thought it might be one of the Nazi leaders' teeth.'

She thought — That's witty.

Then — And seeing things as funny, is being ready to stay alive?

100

A hostess was coming to take their trays. Lilia put down Jason's typescript.

The man said 'You don't believe me.'

She said 'What does it matter what I believe?'

He said 'I could do you a lot of harm.'

Lilia thought — Well, you might also destroy yourself.

The man said 'I don't mind what happens to me.'

She thought — No I'm sure you don't.

He put one of the pills into his mouth: then after a moment took it out again.

She said 'Oh yes, you've got us all in your power.'

She found she did not want to go back to her reading. She thought — There is too much coming in: a white light coming down —

She had her vision again of a hot brown landscape; pale almost blue hills in the distance; a river with green reeds like a thread; a crowd of men and women in white cloaks; a man in a loincloth up to his knees in water. She thought — Well, I know what that is: in the painting you can see his feet through the water. Then the heavens open up and a voice like a bird comes down: and the people in white robes are running, running —

— As if helicopters were after them.

She thought — Now where did that come from?

The man beside her said 'I've killed someone.'

She said 'Oh, have you?'

She thought — Either messages are at random; or if they are messages they tell you something.

He said 'It was in war. In Jerusalem.'

She thought — Oh these wars! which war? the Suez War? the Six Day War? the war between what Jason would call Dr Paragon and the Russian Schoolgirls?

He said 'A boy of about my own age. They'd brought him in for questioning.'

She thought — What is it that people say, that wars are now fought to provide cheap entertainment for television —

The man said ' — The colour of his eyes was the colour of fear — ' Then he laughed.

Lilia said 'You're a Zealot.'

The man said ' — As a matter of fact, I've never been further than Rome — ' Then he laughed again.

Lilia thought — He is in fact mad?

Then — A Zealot is someone who's lost the straight man inside him to let him know he's funny?

The man beside her said 'Yes, I'm a Zealot! I'm a Zealot!' Then — 'What's a Zealot?'

Lilia thought — In that image, in paintings, why is the voice that comes down a bird, and not a child?

She said 'What's going on in Israel now, do you know?'

The man said 'How should I know?'

Lilia said 'Why do people like you want to destroy yourselves?'

The man beside her did not speak for a time: then, when she looked round she saw he had a finger in his mouth and he seemed to be feeling a tooth.

She thought — Dear God, we'll get it down then, like tapioca.

The man said 'Where are you going when you get off the plane?'

She said 'I don't know.' Then — 'To a hotel by the sea.'

She thought — I would not mind if he died?

He said 'I'd like to come too.'

She said 'Of course you can't come too!'

He said 'Why not?'

She thought — Is it wrong, not to care about people who think they have got power over you?

She said 'Look, you think you've got power over us, but you haven't, you haven't!'

He said 'I could hurt your husband.'

She thought — How?

She said 'Who is your partner?'

He said 'Don't you know?' Then — 'Why did you do it?'

She thought — Well, we can deal with all this, can't we, O Jason?

— But this man was beautiful once; there was that small nestling, in its bed of roses.

— Perhaps I will cry?

The voice of the captain came over the loudspeaker saying

that they were flying at such and such an altitude at such and such a speed: how if they looked out of the windows on one side they would see something or other; and if they looked out on the other they would see something different. Lilia thought — But I do not want the aeroplane to land! After all, who wants guilt: who wants battle —

Then — I am in fact afraid I might not manage this?

She said to the man beside her 'Can I have some of your whisky?'

She thought — It is on a tightrope one has power?

The man said 'Oh sure.' He took the whisky out of his bag.

When she was drinking from the bottle Lilia thought — Those dead ashes, as if from a volcano in my mouth —

Then — Might I not be like Judith, with the cut-off head of Holofernes?

The man took the bottle and had a long drink of whisky.

Then Lilia saw her child coming towards her down the aisle.
— With his bright face like a sword and the crowds running, running —

— And a voice coming down —

She said 'I thought I'd lost you!'

He said 'Mummy — '

She said 'Yes?'

He said 'My fly the aeroplane!'

He was waiting to climb over the legs of the man by the aisle. The man was not moving.

The man said 'Let me come with you to your hotel.'

Lilia said to the child 'You fly the aeroplane?'

Her child said 'Yes.'

He was swinging from the arm-rest of the seat of the man by the aisle.

Lilia half stood and leaned over the man to pick up her child. The man put a hand out and felt her behind.

Lilia sat down. She thought — But you won't see, will you, none of this matters.

She said 'Can you lift him over please.'

The man picked up the child and lifted him high as he had done by the metal-detector machine. The child looked down on him like a cherub from a ceiling.

Lilia said 'Put him down.'

She thought — If you hurt my child, you know I'd kill you, don't you.

The man swung the child across and put him on Lilia's lap. In doing so, he let his head rest against her breast.

Lilia thought — He is like a child himself. Then — But it is not by children we are defeated.

She said 'What's Daddy doing?'

Her child said 'Talking.'

Lilia said 'Who to?'

Her child said 'That lady.'

Lilia thought she might say — Oh so that's all right!

Then, holding her child on her knee, she thought — What matters is all we have ever been, all we have ever learned, all we have ever made from ourselves; which are like children —

— Going to and fro, like electricity, in place and time, in imagination —

She said 'What's Daddy saying?'

Her child said 'The aeroplane's not coming down, and he's with the man what thought he'd shot him in that war but hadn't.'

XIII

SCENE: Jotapata, in Galilee: a cellar.

Josephus is with a group of Elders. There is an Old Woman in the background.

Josephus walks up and down as if he were a director on a film set.

The Elders watch him as if they were actors.

From outside there comes an occasional shout or scream, as if the town were being pillaged.

> JOSEPHUS
> — Death to the enemy without! —
> ELDERS
> — Death to the enemy without! —
> JOSEPHUS
> — Death to the traitor within! —
> ELDERS
> — Death to the traitor within! —
> JOSEPHUS
> Till we're all in one room —

The Elders look uncertain.

> JOSEPHUS
> In a cellar. In Jotapata.

He glances into the camera.

Then he goes to one of the Elders and leads him out in front of the others.

> JOSEPHUS
> The Romans have broken in.
> The town is being pillaged.
> Women and children are being killed.
>
> Now you're not going to let them just do that, are you?

He stands back and looks at the Elder. He shouts —

JOSEPHUS

— Death is our bride! —

FIRST ELDER

— Death is our bride! —

JOSEPHUS

— But don't be taken in! —

FIRST ELDER

— Don't be taken in! —

Josephus murmurs —

JOSEPHUS

On a dark night, can you tell the difference?

FIRST ELDER

On a dark night —

He watches Josephus uncertainly.

Josephus glances into the camera.

Then he walks round as if despairingly.

JOSEPHUS

A little more passion please! You're doing something
terrible after all! Killing yourselves! Of your own free
will! No one's making you. People have always been
doing it —

He comes back to the First Elder. He acts —

JOSEPHUS

— Lord God, remember me, I pray thee, and strengthen
me, I pray thee —

The First Elder watches him as if hypnotised.

JOSEPHUS

The Philistines have broken in! Women and children
are being killed! You're chained between two pillars,
like the donkey between two bundles of hay —

— Will you look heroic? —

— Will you look ridiculous? —

He goes and takes a knife from a Second Elder.

He murmurs —

JOSEPHUS

As a matter of fact, you'll look ridiculous anyway —
But no one will mind that if you're dead.
It's called heroic.

He comes with the knife and gives it to the First Elder.

JOSEPHUS

Now, what are your feelings? You've made a pact. You don't want to break a pact. You might get stuck underneath it, like ice.

He goes to the Second Elder and takes him out of the group and places him in front of the First Elder with his back to him.

Then he stands back. He murmurs —

JOSEPHUS

— Nothing can be done against moral or religious principles —

Then he shouts —

JOSEPHUS

— He's got your knife! —

SECOND ELDER

He's got my knife?

Josephus turns to the First Elder.

JOSEPHUS

— You're not going to let him get away with that, are you?

The two Elders watch him uncertainly.

JOSEPHUS

You'd better kill him first.

Before he kills you.

He goes to the First Elder and raises the hand with the knife in it.

JOSEPHUS

That's good business.

That's only sensible —

Two people can't be in the same place at the same time —

He stands back.

JOSEPHUS

It's always the first that's the hardest —

Like the first hundred thousand.

After that it's easy.

You have guilt.

He waits.

JOSEPHUS

Guilt. Gilt.

He's got what you want —

And you know where that is —

Inside him.

The First Elder stabs the Second Elder, who screams and falls to the ground.

JOSEPHUS

That's right.

Or shall we do it again?

Oh no, we can't.

Unless we're in the same place at the same time — on a stage.

We're the same person.

He glances into the camera.

Then he walks round again.

JOSEPHUS

— So what can we do? —

— One and one makes two! —

— Take another person!

He takes hold of a Third Elder.

Then he stops and stares at the Old Woman at the back of the set.

JOSEPHUS

And where do you live?

The Old Woman looks round as if she might have forgotten her lines.

OLD WOMAN

Above the theatre?

Josephus frowns at her. Then he leads the Third Elder out and places him behind the First.

JOSEPHUS

We've got to have justice, you see.

We're not in the Garden now, you know.

Not in a — metaphor.

Not in some sort of — fairy-story.

He takes the knife from the First Elder and gives it to

the Third.

Then he waits.

After a time the Old Woman speaks from the back.

OLD WOMAN

And one times one makes —

JOSEPHUS

What —

OLD WOMAN

It's a matter of language: subject, verb, subject —

JOSEPHUS

Not billiard balls? —

OLD WOMAN

Waves —

JOSEPHUS

Particles.

Josephus watches the two Elders.

After a time —

JOSEPHUS

Haven't you read Aristotle?

Billiard balls —

Are the form and function of society.

The Third Elder screams and stabs the First Elder, who falls.

JOSEPHUS

It goes on all the time —

OLD WOMAN

It goes through you.

Josephus goes and takes a Fourth Elder from the group. He places him behind the Third Elder.

JOSEPHUS

It's an endless belt. Do you know the story of the endless belt? Well, there was this man, see, and it was his job to run up and down underneath an escalator —

The Old Woman puts her head in her hands.

JOSEPHUS

— And to catch the steps as they came out at the bottom and to run with them again to the top. Well, someone said to him —

He raises the hand of the Fourth Elder.

JOSEPHUS

— I thought it was an endless belt! —

He stands back and watches the two Elders.

JOSEPHUS

— And the man said: Well, so it is!

There I am, belting from the bottom to the top and back again —

The Fourth Elder acts stabbing the Third Elder, who screams and falls.

The Old Woman takes her hands away from her eyes. She seems to have been laughing.

OLD WOMAN

But he didn't have the knife!

JOSEPHUS

Who didn't have the knife?

He goes and looks down at the body of the Third Elder. He acts as if shocked.

JOSEPHUS

You mean, he was acting?

He comes back to the Old Woman. He murmurs —

JOSEPHUS

Escalator is a Latin word —

The Old Woman says loudly —

OLD WOMAN

It was when he heard the joke —

JOSEPHUS

It was he who screamed —

OLD WOMAN

It was when he heard me say: It goes through you —

Josephus glances into the camera.

JOSEPHUS

See if you can find it.

The Old Woman goes and looks under the body of the Third Elder. She comes back to Josephus with the knife.

OLD WOMAN

It's when you go in and out of context —

110

JOSEPHUS

What else did he say?

OLD WOMAN

Who?

JOSEPHUS

Him. The other. The one in Galilee.

OLD WOMAN

— What is dead comes alive —

JOSEPHUS

And —

OLD WOMAN

— Don't tell anyone.

JOSEPHUS

God, if you think I'm telling anyone!

He glances into the camera.

Then he turns to the group of Elders. He beckons to a
Fifth Elder.

JOSEPHUS

We can't stand around here all day. Time is money.
Money's running out. The Romans have broken in. The
body politic is being pillaged. Are you going to let them
rape your ten-year-old daughter?

He places the Fifth Elder behind the Fourth Elder.

He seems uncertain whether or not to give him the knife.

JOSEPHUS

I've never really understood about that.

OLD WOMAN

What?

JOSEPHUS

The ten-year-old daughter.

OLD WOMAN

I think it's because they want to rape their own
daughters.

JOSEPHUS

I thought it was more they thought they'd raped their
mothers.

OLD WOMAN

But they hadn't.

111

JOSEPHUS

— So we can't stand around here all day?

He hands the knife to the Fifth Elder, who raises his arm.
Josephus stands back and watches the two Elders.

OLD WOMAN

It's like eeny meeny miny mo —

JOSEPHUS

But that depends where you begin.

OLD WOMAN

Well, where did we?

After a time the Fifth Elder stabs the Fourth Elder, who
screams and falls.

JOSEPHUS

With a bang —

OLD WOMAN

And then?

JOSEPHUS

Things follow —

OLD WOMAN

How does anyone get away?

JOSEPHUS

Perhaps you can't answer that.

OLD WOMAN

It just happens —

JOSEPHUS

Well it does; or does or doesn't it?

He goes and looks at the body of the Third Elder.
He pokes it with his toe.

OLD WOMAN

You needn't quite believe it!

JOSEPHUS

— Which would be in line with the best contemporary
thought —

The Old Woman puts her head in her hands.

JOSEPHUS

Sextus Empiricus! Heraclitus!

He goes to the group and takes from it a Sixth Elder.
He places him behind the Fifth Elder, as if wearily.

The Old Woman looks up.

OLD WOMAN

What I don't understand is, why they never ask themselves —

JOSEPHUS

Who?

OLD WOMAN

Oh no, they're not the same person.

Josephus takes the knife from the hand of the Fifth Elder and gives it to the Sixth Elder.

OLD WOMAN

It's like a ballet.

JOSEPHUS

A belt?

OLD WOMAN

A ballet!

JOSEPHUS

— What is a belt, mixed, with learner in the middle —

The Old Woman puts her head in her hands.

Josephus raises the Sixth Elder's hand with the knife. He stands back.

The Old Woman looks up.

OLD WOMAN

But who are we then?

JOSEPHUS

I thought you said you lived above the theatre.

OLD WOMAN

We can't hear them —

JOSEPHUS

Perhaps they can't hear us —

He looks into the camera.

OLD WOMAN

Why, what are we saying?

JOSEPHUS

What will you do with the children?

OLD WOMAN

Say we've killed them.

The Sixth Elder stabs the Fifth Elder who falls, screaming.

113

Josephus leaves the Elders and comes forward.

JOSEPHUS

Well, I don't think it makes sense exactly. Talk is a context.

OLD WOMAN

You watch it?

JOSEPHUS

You think it'll work?

OLD WOMAN

— We're standing, with the children, on those battlements at Masada —

JOSEPHUS

— The Romans are about to break in —

The Old Woman points to the Third Elder.

OLD WOMAN

That one's still alive —

JOSEPHUS

Someone, in another time, another place, will hear us?

XIV

Jason had first met Lilia when they had been taken to a theatre by mutual friends. Lilia had arrived only just before the curtain had gone up, so that Jason's first view of her had been along a row of stalls. He saw a girl with an absolutely open face — like the stuff of flowers, he thought, before petals are stamped on them. Then — But this openness, is it a sign of wanting to learn or of cracking up? or of both, a cocoon and a butterfly. The lights in the auditorium went out. He thought — At least she is pretty.

The play was a fashionable one in which the central character was a psychiatrist who complained how hopeless everything was: how he felt his patients were better than he since at least they were in touch with their feelings even if these, like everything else, resulted in misery. Jason hated the play. He thought — The audience likes it because they are thus reassured about their own dreadful feelings; and misery. Then — If I were not trapped by my own cowardice would I not jump onto the stage and denounce the play? like Hamlet into the grave; and come alive for my curtain call at the end of the last act. But then I would not be able to spin my webs to catch this pretty girl; for if she is a butterfly, I am a spider.

Looking along the rows of stalls again he saw her leaning forwards and frowning intently. He thought — She is waiting for someone to catch her? or for honey?

Jason knew that their mutual friends, a husband and a wife, were probably doing some matchmaking in asking him and Lilia to the play. Jason had been living apart from his first wife for some time, and he had recently broken with the girl he had been living with in Rome. Lilia, he had been told, was involved with a man much older than herself, who was at the moment on a lecture tour in Italy.

During the interval Jason wondered if he should say what he felt about the play; then he thought — This girl must have had enough of men who chase after rags like bulls in the intervals of plays: what she needs is something mysterious, like honey.

The husband and wife said how much they loved the play. The girl said — Yes, she loved it too. But her voice seemed to have little to do with what she was saying. Jason thought — She is either slightly daft or enlightened: enlightenment being knowing how to use being-slightly-daft's appearance.

Going out of the theatre at the end of the play he walked slightly behind the girl and wondered whether or not he should take her arm. He thought — Will she know I am wondering this? The husband said 'What did you make of the play?' Jason said 'I hated it.' The girl did not seem to hear. Jason thought — Does one know what one is looking for in an experiment? The girl waited just ahead of him on the pavement. Her profile, what he could see of it, seemed to glisten with rain.

In the car — they were being driven back for supper to the house where the girl was staying — an argument got under way between Jason and the husband and the wife. — Why did you hate the play? — Because it makes people so pleased with their own miseries — But if it's true? — But you can make what you like to be true — But what about *King Lear*? — What about *King Lear*? — You can say that about *King Lear* — Yes I do say that about *King Lear* —

The girl, sitting in the front seat by the husband, still seemed to be being driven like the figurehead of a ship through spray or rain.

When they were in the house that had been lent to the girl by friends she moved in and out of the kitchen still managing to keep her back to him. Jason thought — To see her full-face, would one have to pick her like a flower? While she prepared supper the husband and wife continued their argument with him —

— But the point of *King Lear* is that people can come to terms with miseries —

— Yes, people do indeed come to terms with miseries; what they can't do is —

— But God, that would be boring! —

— Yes that's what I'm saying —

— What? —

— That coming to terms with happiness, God, wouldn't people say that was boring! —

Then when they moved into the kitchen and were settling round a small scrubbed table the girl suddenly faced him and seemed to stand to attention and said, as if she were a child on a stage who had never before acted — 'I've never heard so much rubbish in all my life!'

Jason thought — Well that's all right!

The girl had brown skin, pale hair, almost black eyes, a short upper lip, large mouth —

He thought — Is it that heroine in Tolstoy who has a short upper lip?

He said 'Why?'

She said 'I don't know why, do things have to be why, it just is rubbish!'

He thought — Well, that really is all right.

She banged about at the stove. She produced very good cucumber soup. Then beef like flowers.

She and the husband and the wife began to talk about mutual acquaintances.

Jason thought — She uses words like a line with a hook on the end, to go fishing with in her unconscious.

After supper they continued to gossip for a time. Jason joined in with his own funny stories about friends. Then when the time came for people to go —

— He had been thinking: Dear God, the rituals one goes through in order to find out what is in one's unconscious —

— And the girl's eyes had been searching behind his from time to time as if she might or might not find there what was on the hook on the end of her line —

When the time came for them to go, Jason hung about in the hall while the husband and wife fetched their coats and made arrangements with the girl for a further meeting.

And Jason picked up from a table in the hall a picture post-card which was of Mary and Joseph and the infant Jesus going across a desert on a donkey —

— And he thought — I know that painting! It is by Giotto, and is at Assisi —

— And then the girl, who was called Lilia, stood beside him and said 'You don't have to go.'

He said 'Ah, one never knows!'

She moved away from him.

Then when the husband and wife had driven away: pleased, Jason hoped, at the success of their matchmaking —

— Lilia closed the door of the flat, lit a cigarette, and backed away as if smoke were coming after her. She said —

'What do you mean, one never knows?'

He said 'I mean, one never knows about anything of importance.'

She said 'You think this is important?'

They sat either side of an unlit stove. They occasionally held out their hands to it.

She said 'I thought you knew everything.'

Then — 'You were putting on such an act!'

He thought — But Lilia, you see, if I do not say anything for a time, it is because I can't think of anything to say, as well as its being an act.

She said 'What did you mean when you said that a really grown-up sort of play would be if everyone, actors and audience, knew that what they said was rubbish?'

He thought — Good Lord, did I say that?

He said 'I think I meant, that sort of play would be if everyone knew that what was said and heard was said and heard as actors and audience.'

She said 'Why?'

He said 'Because that would be true.'

She said 'Putting on a performance — '

He said 'But you put on a performance anyway. But in this case you'd know what you were doing.'

'And did you?'

'You might get what you want.'

'And what did you want?'

He said 'You.'

118

He thought — Well, that might be true.

Then, as she stared at him — What she is searching for is some sort of future like a fortune teller with entrails.

She said 'You manipulate people — '

He said 'So do you.'

She said 'I don't succeed.'

He said 'No, I meant it, one never knows about anything of importance.'

She said again 'You think this important?'

She stubbed out her cigarette as if it were against someone's eyes.

Then she said 'I don't go to bed with people I like.'

He thought he might say — Where do you do it then?

He said 'Then that's all right.'

She said 'Why is it all right?'

He said 'Because if you like me we won't go to bed, and if you don't we will.'

After a time she said 'And either way's all right?'

He said 'Yes.'

She said 'I see.'

She lit another cigarette. He thought — It is some terrible beast, or breast, coming after her: that she is trying to set on fire.

She said 'And this is what grown-up people know if they know they are actors — '

He said 'Yes.'

She said 'But if you knew you wanted to get me — '

He said 'I didn't know if I would.'

She said 'Do you mean that?'

He said 'Yes.'

He thought — There is something happening here beyond a girl who wants both to have her cake and to run away from it —

She said 'I don't go to bed with people I like because I suppose it would be — '

He said 'What — '

He thought — She leaves the ends of her sentences open so that it is this that is like a hook that goes down to drag up entrails —

She said ' — terrifying.'

Then — 'You were looking at that postcard.'

He said 'Yes, you know the painting?'

He thought — It is her lover, who is too old for her, who has sent her that postcard of Mary and the child from Assisi?

He said 'But you do go to bed with — '

She said 'Who?'

He said 'Who sent you that postcard?'

She left the stove and went to the table in the hall and came back with the postcard. She turned it over. She read ' — I've lit a candle — '

Then she sat down and began to cry.

Jason said 'I thought he was in Rome.'

She said 'Well, he went to Assisi.'

Then she sat up and stopped crying.

Jason thought — I'm tired. Do I in fact care whether or not we go to bed together?

She said 'Yes of course I go to bed with him.'

He said 'Don't you like him then?'

She said 'That's different.'

He thought — Why?

Then — Did she say love: or like?

Then — For God's sake, he lit a candle: she wants a baby?

Then — Why did I think that?

He said 'Let's go upstairs.'

He thought — You jump: you don't know why you jump.

Then — She doesn't have a baby with her lover?

Then again — Why did I think that.

She said 'You want to?' She looked disappointed.

He said 'I'll sit on the end of your bed.'

She said 'What would be the point of that?'

He said 'Then sooner or later I'll fall either off, or into it, won't I, as if from a tightrope.'

She went ahead of him up the stairs. He thought — Dear God, and with an arse like that —

Then — At least this is funny.

He said 'Of course it's terrifying to go to bed with people one likes. Why else are there all these daft systems of morality?'

She said 'You mean nowadays it's so easy?'

In her bedroom he lay on the end of the bed and put his hands underneath his head and stared at the ceiling. He thought — In this small hot room, like a hotel on the edge of the desert —

— Is that a cherub in the corner of the ceiling?

She said 'You've got a wife? A girlfriend?'

He said 'Yes.'

She said 'Which?'

He said 'Both.'

She went through to the bathroom. She said 'Is that why you never know what's going to happen with anything of importance?'

He thought — That's witty.

Then — Well indeed, there is something out of the ordinary happening here: a bird, or voice, waiting to come down from the ceiling —

He called out — 'Do you know the story of the Zen master with his stick?'

She said 'Yes.'

He said 'You do?'

He thought — This is impossible.

She came to the door of the bathroom. She held a small towel in front of her. She said 'The master says to his pupil — If you say I am holding this stick I will hit you with it, and if you do not say I am holding this stick I will hit you with it — '

He said 'How do you know that?'

She said 'My brother's always going on about it.'

He said 'Oh, you've got a brother have you?'

He thought — And a body like that!

She went back into the bathroom.

He sat up and began to take off his shoes.

She called — 'What are you going to do?'

He said ' — And the thing for the pupil to do is to snatch the stick from the Zen master and so put the whole thing into a different context — '

When he was undressed he got into bed. He lay on his back and looked at the ceiling.

He thought — Dear God, she might in fact want a baby.

She came in from the bathroom and stood by the edge of the bed. She was wearing a nightdress. She said 'Look, I must tell you — '

He said 'It's all right, I think I know.'

She said 'How can you possibly know?'

He thought — I am mad: what will I do? Instead of the stick, be left holding the —

After a time she said 'I thought you never knew about anything of importance.'

He said 'Ah, but you said that was all rubbish anyway.'

She said 'Oh God I do like you!'

He said 'We can love too?'

She took off her nightdress.

He thought — Dear God, in this context!

She got into bed.

He said 'And what do you do with your lovers, do you chuck them out before morning?'

She said 'And what do you do with your wife and girlfriend, do you fuck them at the same time?'

He thought — And there is that candle burning at Assisi!

XV

Lilia paused at the entrance to the first-class compartment of
the aeroplane and thought — This strange world! with its
spaced-out chairs and quiet loneliness: the door open to the
captain's cabin beyond: the controls of the aeroplane which
my child says he has been flying: is this one of the worlds that
we are told do not exist except when we are observing them?

She said 'Hullo.'

Jason said 'Hullo.'

She thought she might say — I wonder if you remember me.

Jason said 'We were just talking about you!'

Lilia said 'Oh, what were you saying?'

Jason said 'Jane. My wife Lilia.'

The girl beside Jason said 'Hullo.'

Lilia said 'How do you do.'

Jason said 'I was saying how you'd said you didn't always see
the point of my characters behaving like they do: standing back
from themselves; watching; acting.'

Lilia said 'In your script or in real life?'

Jason said 'Both.'

Then — 'Like that they wouldn't be trapped: by themselves,
or by others.'

Lilia said 'Can I sit here?'

Jason said 'Yes do.'

Lilia sat down in the seat on the left across the aisle from
Jason. She thought — He has now got what he likes: a woman
on either side of him talking about his work.

Jane said 'They're a sort of demonstration — '

Jason said 'Yes.'

Jane said 'And people would either see it or they wouldn't.'

Jason said 'Quite.'

Jane said 'Not they'd see they were either acting or not, but they might see they were both. I mean, they'd either see this or they wouldn't.'

Lilia said 'Or both.' She laughed. Then — 'But how far back can you go?'

Jason said 'I think that's about as far.' Then — 'I think that's how things actually work.'

Lilia thought — Well, have you made your demonstration about how, for the sake of making a proper film, the film can't be made?

Jane said 'And that's how you get out?'

Jason said 'Get out of what — '

Jane said 'Whatever you're in.'

Lilia thought — Well now I'm here, in this strange world beyond the steward's cabin, what do I make of it? There's that huge man in front of me, I suppose he's Epstien, he seems to be reaching up for shadows like a baby towards the ceiling; there's that woman, Lisa something or other, who's staggering across the aisle as if drunk; there's that actor in the front on the right — good God, is he, what's his name, the boyfriend?

Jane was saying 'But the trouble is about people being like this in 66 A.D.'

Jason said 'But they knew an extraordinary amount in 66 A.D.: there was a lot going on: things could have gone one way or the other: or both! There were all these people beginning to see that individuals had to be responsible; that things like empires and churches and even gods were in some way fairy-stories; but they might be necessary fairy-stories for everyone to stay alive by; so this sort of knowledge had to be somewhat secret, there was no language to describe it, language was to do with fairy-stories.'

Jane said 'But they were defeated.'

Lilia thought — And we want to win.

Jason said 'But perhaps that was a fairy-story that they were defeated, so they could stay alive.'

'With the other people sitting on the secret — '

' — To keep it warm.'

Jane laughed, staring at Jason.

Lilia thought — All right: but this girl will not cook for you, live for you, have your child, O Jason —

Her child seemed to be trying to turn somersaults over the arm-rest of the seat at the front on the left.

A man with spectacles had appeared with the steward and was standing over Epstien. He was saying 'I thought he should have oxygen.' The steward was saying 'Does he usually have oxygen?' The man with the spectacles was saying 'Oh yes, he usually has oxygen.' The steward reached up to the locker in the rack above Epstien's head. Lilia thought — They are talking about him as if he were a fish.

Jane said 'But they didn't know about all the connections in space and time.'

Jason said 'But there were all those mystics.'

Jane said 'But isn't what you're talking about science?'

Jason said 'It's all coming round: eating its own tail again.'

Lilia thought — That oxygen mask being lowered above Epstien's head is like an umbilical cord.

Jane was saying 'There was a chance of Jews being Christians? Of Christians being Jews?

Jason said 'Or both.'

Jane said 'And that was the point of that bird flying around — '

Lilia said 'Oh yes, what is all this about the aeroplane not coming down?'

Jason looked at her. It was as if he were suddenly blinded. Lilia thought — Someone has been telling him about the man in the lavatory?

Jason said 'They're having trouble at Tel Aviv airport.'

Jane said 'You mean, the bird does not come down?'

Lilia thought — War has been declared?

Jason said 'What?' Then — 'That bird first out of the ark?' Then — 'That other bird?'

Lilia thought — Would we stop talking like this if war were declared?

She said 'What sort of trouble?'

Jason said 'We don't know.' Then — 'We may have to be diverted.'

The man with spectacles was looking down at Lilia curiously.

She thought — He is their nanny? Another boyfriend? He also knows about the —

Then — He is the man who thought he'd shot Jason in that war?

Wolf Tanner called — 'Let's have some more champagne!'

Lisa Grant said 'Eat, drink and be merry!'

The man with spectacles said 'Comfy?'

He was talking to Epstien, but seemed to be looking at Lilia.

Lilia thought — Really, that oxygen mask being put over Epstien's face is like the wet towel of a torturer.

Then — Where is my child?

Jane said 'Do you think the Israelis are doing it again?'

Jason said 'Doing what again?'

Jane said 'Destroying themselves.'

Lilia wanted to say — Do you think we're not doing this?

The head of her child appeared over the top of the seats at the front on the left. He was staring at the pipe going down to the oxygen mask over Epstien's face.

Lilia thought — The man from the tourist-class will suddenly appear at the door and say: I wonder if you remember me —

She said 'What did you have to eat?'

Jason said 'Caviare and champagne.'

She said 'I knew it!'

Jane said 'If we crash, we'll be the first to be eaten!'

Lilia thought — Oh yes, we're cannibals!

Her child was stretching out towards Epstien's pipe or umbilical cord: he began to stroke it, gently.

The man with spectacles said 'If you two have stopped having it off — '

He was looking at Lilia; but seemed also to be talking to Jane who was next to Jason.

He said ' — Perhaps you can think of doing something about reservations.'

Jane said 'Reservations?'

The man with the spectacles said to Jane 'Or you might get fired too.'

Lilia thought — Are you fired? Jason?

Jane said 'But how can I do anything about reservations

when I don't know where we're going?'

Jason said 'Scientifically, can you even if you do?'

The plane gave a lurch. Jason acted clutching at the arm-rests of his seat. Jane began laughing.

Lilia said 'Have you been fired?'

Jason said 'Apparently.'

The man with the spectacles said 'They can't hit us from here.'

Lisa Grant had begun crying.

The man with spectacles said 'We're over the sea.'

Lilia said 'Who is that man?'

Jason said 'He's the man who thought he'd shot me in that war — '

Jane said 'But hadn't.'

Lilia said 'You were over the sea?'

A hostess was coming down the aisle pouring champagne. Lilia and Jason and Jane were laughing so much that the hostess almost went past them. Jason called out — 'And a glass for my wife here!'

Epstien, in the seat in front of Lilia, took the oxygen mask away from his face and said 'Have these people got tickets to the first-class?'

The child took hold of the pipe to the oxygen mask.

Lilia went and picked up her child and carried him back to her seat opposite Jason. She held him on her knee.

Epstien said 'Get them out of here!'

The hostess had filled up Jason's glass. He handed it to Lilia. The hostess filled up Jane's glass. She handed it to Jason.

Jason called — 'And a glass please for my friend here!'

Epstien, holding the oxygen mask like a handkerchief in front of his face, leaned round in his seat towards Jason and said 'You won't work in films again.'

Jason clutched at the sides of his seat as if fearfully. He said 'But they've got boats with rockets on the sea!'

Lilia said 'I thought those sorts of boats were under the sea.'

Jane said 'And what they're working on now, is how to get them up on to dry land.'

Jason and Lilia were laughing so much that they spilt some of their champagne.

127

Wolf Tanner, in the seat on the right in front, turned, leaned round into the aisle, and looked first at Jason, then at the child, then at Lilia.

Lilia thought — That's not a bad face: he and the other man are some sort of mirror-images of themselves: perhaps that's why they have to put rings round each other's cocks: to know who they are: or, as if they were similar poles of a magnet, to stop them repelling one another.

Wolf Tanner said 'How do you do.'

Lilia said 'How do you do.'

Wolf Tanner said 'I don't think we've met.'

Lilia wondered if she should say — I've met your partner.

Jason put his head into the aisle and said 'Wolf — '

Wolf Tanner said 'Yes?'

There was the famous smile: one corner of the mouth going up higher than the other.

Jason said 'When we land at the airport, if we ever do, and the whole place is surrounded by men with machine guns — '

Lisa Grant cried 'We're going to be diverted!'

Jason said ' — Or when we land in some lonely desert, and the whole world is filled by armies with suicide pacts — '

A hostess was standing over Lisa Grant again and saying 'Drink this.'

Spud was saying 'Not with commodores.'

Wolf Tanner was saying 'No commodores with drinkies.'

Jason said ' — Couldn't you — you must have played this a hundred times, Wolf — come down the steps of the aeroplane like one of those lonely gunfighters — '

Lilia thought — O Jason, you think you can do it like this?

Jason said ' — And then you could be shot, you know, just as you were about to reach the airport building; and then Lisa could come out running, running, and you could die in her arms — '

His child said 'Daddy, are you drunk?'

Jason said 'Yes.'

' — And so we could all leave the theatre, or the airport building, or whatever, and go home.'

Wolf Tanner stared at him.

Lilia thought — You think, in the real world, we might be

saved by this sort of thing?

Wolf Tanner said 'You mean, create a diversion.'

Jason said 'Yes.'

Jane said 'You mean, like *The Petrified Forest*.'

Jason said 'Yes like *The Petrified Forest*!'

Jane said 'Have you seen *The Petrified Forest*?'

Wolf Tanner said 'I am the Petrified Forest!'

Lisa Grant said 'Where Humphrey Bogart rushes out and dies in Bette Davis' arms — '

Spud said 'It wasn't Humphrey Bogart — '

Lisa Grant said 'Who was it then?'

Lilia said 'Leslie Howard.'

Jason said 'Where Leslie Howard rushes out and dies in Humphrey Bogart's arms — '

Jane said 'Humphrey Bogart was the gangster.'

Wolf Tanner said 'But he wasn't creating a diversion — '

Jason said 'No this is the diversion.'

Epstien said 'Spud — '

Spud said 'Yes?'

Epstien said 'Will you get those fucking people out of here?'

Jason said ' — And then Epstien can come exploding out of the side of the plane like that man in that film, what was its name — '

Lilia was laughing so much that champagne went up her nose. She thought — Oh Jason, Jason, I will never again not trust you!

Then she said 'I'm sorry.'

Jason said 'Sorry about what?'

She said 'Have you really been fired?'

Jason seemed to think for a time. Then he said 'I've managed to get this special diversion, you see, so we can go straight to our hotel by the Red Sea.'

Then Lilia said 'I'm frightened.'

He said 'Frightened about what?'

She thought — Perhaps for our child: who carries such messages from the unconscious to the conscious: who is with his family and their donkey going across a desert to the Red Sea.

Jason said 'None of the frightening stuff matters.'

She wanted to say — But tell me again what does.

Jane said to Jason 'That's why you wrote it like that?'

129

Jason said 'Wrote it like what?'

Jane said 'With all the connections. Seeing. With things always happening elsewhere.'

Lilia said 'What things.'

Jane said 'You trust it works?'

Jason said 'How do you know about all this?'

Jane said 'Oh, I knew about you.'

Jason said 'How?'

Jane said 'I've told you. I know a friend of yours.'

Lilia thought — Oh talk to me!

Jason said to Jane 'And where will you go, when you're out of it, by your Red Sea?'

Lilia thought — Perhaps he is telling something to me.

Then Wolf Tanner said 'Hullo, partner.'

He was looking towards the back of the first-class compartment where someone had come in.

Lilia thought — Ah now, here is that man with death about him like a lonely gunfighter!

Jane was saying 'But you've still got to win.'

Jason said 'Oh yes you've got to win.'

Then Jane looked past him and said 'Hullo, Julius — '

Lilia thought — He is called Julius.

Julius, in the doorway, said 'Don't move anyone!'

Wolf Tanner said 'Have you been enjoying yourself?'

Julius said 'This is a stick-up!'

Epstien said 'Yes I'm sure it was!'

Epstien was twisting back over the top of his seat and grinning.

Wolf Tanner had turned to his front and was staring at the wall.

Lilia thought — What things are happening elsewhere?

Julius seemed to be waiting for her to move her legs so he could sit beside her by the window.

Jane stood and moved into the aisle, as if to make room for Lilia beside Jason.

Jason moved to the seat by the window.

Jane said 'Well, the Romans are breaking in. There are those children at Masada.'

XVI

Masada is a rock a thousand feet high in the desert. On one side there are mountains as high as the rock but separated from it by deep ravines: on the other the ground drops away to the Dead Sea. The top of Masada is a plateau six hundred yards long and two hundred wide. Here people have come for centuries to live and build fortresses and palaces and hermitages in which they can feel cut off from the world; and the world, as if in some envy of them, has tried to break in.

There are now three ways up from the valley to the top of Masada. The first is the old path which defenders and kings and hermits used — a path which is easy to guard from the top, since it winds like a serpent up the rock-face and stones can be hurled down on it. The second way is the huge earth-and-stone ramp that the Romans built when they broke into Masada. And the third is the modern cable-car which takes tourists to the top and then down again in one day. No one now wants to live on Masada: it is as if the world, having finally broken in, had destroyed the point of anyone staying there.

There is conceivably a fourth way to the top up the southern cliff-face: but this can be attempted only by expert climbers.

One of the young men guarding Masada at this time — Masada has become something of a national shrine in Israel, and although no one wants to settle there, in this age of psychological rather than of total warfare it is thought that it still might be an object of attack by Israel's enemies — one of the young men guarding Masada at this time was David Kahn, a student of psychology. He was a recent arrival from the West in Israel: he had taken his degree at Tel Aviv University and was now doing his military service. His job was to keep an eye on the parties of schoolchildren and tourists being taken round Masada: to see that there was no one amongst them who might plant a bomb or take out a gun or do anything else that might break in as it were symbolically upon this symbol of defiant Israel.

David Kahn knew well the history of Masada: he had read Josephus' account in *The Jewish War* of the mass suicide of the Zealots: he had also read Josephus' later long and painstaking defence of Judaism, which was rarely studied by people of his generation. He knew how strongly Josephus was held in contempt by Jews: also how strongly he, Josephus, had wished to justify Judaism. As David Kahn listened from time to time to Josephus' own story of the siege being read out to the school-children at the top of Masada he wondered about Josephus' claim that it was he, and not those who had killed themselves honourably, who represented the true interests of Judaism — it being the task of the Jews to promulgate God's word, and not to maintain their identity through disasters or stories of disaster.

David Kahn sat on a stone on the top of Masada. He held a sub-machine gun on his knee. He also held a book from which, from time to time, he read a few paragraphs. He thought — I am to some extent still a stranger in this landscape: I will be just as alert outside, doing my duty, if I am alert inside, reading.

He read —

> The whole of creation, animate and inanimate, is held in the throes of a universal struggle for redemption from the evil which has entered the world, and for the restoration of that harmony in which the whole will find salvation in the establishment of the kingdom of God.
>
> The pivot around which Jewish mysticism revolves is the conception of man as a being created to be a co-worker with God; and, as such, endowed with the capacity and power to control and influence things towards his own ends as well as towards the fulfilment of creation. What is distinctive in Jewish mysticism is its claim to be in possession of the secrets of the *modus operandi* of this co-operative activity with the divine, and thereby able to make the human contribution all the more effective.

At some distance from David Kahn there was a group of school-children having read out to them Josephus' story of the last stand of the Zealots. David Kahn thought — It is the fact of its being Josephus' story that is still read out, rather than the events it describes, that is representative of the secrets of the modus operandi of man as co-worker with God?

He thought he would go and look up an extract from another book he had been reading, which extract he had written down in a notebook he kept in his hut. The book was to do with modern physics; the hut was where David Kahn and the six men under his command were based on the top of Masada. He thought — I understand why men should prefer death to dishonour because this is the way that men now exist as social animals: what I do not understand is how the unit of society seems to have been taken as the same for thousands of years.

Groups of tourists were swarming among the rocks: some Japanese were holding their cameras to their eyes like guns. David Kahn thought — The world has been changed by bits of information exploding like bullets: has anyone noticed that it has also been changed by us noticing this?

The hut was inside a building which had once been used by Zealots: later by Christian hermits. Some scrolls had been found there from the time of the Essenes. David Kahn found his notebook. He sat down in the shadows. He thought — This is what a religious activity should be: something that goes on distinct from, yet at the centre of, the systems of a society.

He read —

> When an observation on the system is made in one region the wave function changes instantly, not only in that region, but also in far-away regions. This behaviour is completely natural for a function that describes probabilities, for probabilities depend upon what is known about the system, and if knowledge changes as a result of an observation, then the probability function (the amplitude of the wave function squared) should change. In quantum theory this collapse of the wave function is such that what *happens* in a far-away place must, in some cases, depend

on what an observer here chooses to observe; what you see there depends on what I *do* here. This is a completely non-classical non-local effect.

David Kahn thought — Well, yes.

Then — What do I mean, well yes?

— I must ask my wife.

David Kahn's wife had taken her degree in physics: she was now a security official at Lod airport near Tel Aviv.

Going back to where he had been sitting on the rock David Kahn thought — But what I mean is, what unit of society is there, except the whole?

— It is our knowledge that this is so that might affect things?

He looked round for the other men who were on duty with him on Masada. They were seven in all: they were in radio contact with a helicopter station a few minutes' flight away. He thought — But are we not now in Israel in something of the position of the Jews at the time of Josephus? We are surrounded by people who want to destroy us: we still do not believe that the unit of society is the whole.

He watched a girl going past who was courier to a group of tourists. He knew her slightly. He thought — Shall I try to make a date with her at the guest house behind the cable-car station after duty? Would that be, or not be, since I am married, treating society as a whole?

Then — There are also all those Israelis now settling in the lands where they have been asked by our government not to settle: who thus play into the hands of those who want to destroy us.

— Is it yourselves you destroy, if you do not recognise the whole?

A small figure — that of a tourist? — appeared running over the horizon to the south of the plateau on the top of Masada.

David Kahn thought — A recognition of any society less than the whole involves itself necessarily with a need for killing and self-sacrifice and betrayal —

He heard the voice of the girl courier coming down on the wind, reading out to her group of tourists the speech of

Eleazar, the leader of the Zealots at the time of their mass suicide, as related by Josephus —

> Ever since primitive man began to think, the words of our ancestors and of the gods, supported by the actions and spirit of our forefathers, have constantly impressed on us that life is the calamity for man, not death. Death gives freedom to our souls and lets them depart to their own pure home where they will know nothing of any calamity; but while they are confined within a mortal body and share its miseries, in strict truth they are dead. For association of the divine with the mortal is most improper —

David Kahn wanted to shout — But that wasn't what we were told!

Then — Was it?

— Were, or were not, Jews told that to the whole lump they had to be the leaven?

The ground curved away on the top of Masada going down to the southern bastion. The figure that had appeared over the horizon seemed to have found, and to be talking to, one of David Kahn's men.

David Kahn thought — Two hundred yards, open fire —

Then — Probably a child has fallen into one of the underground caverns or cisterns.

Or — There are those dissident groups who seem to be working for the self-destruction of Israel; who have threatened to make some demonstration at Masada.

More figures came running over the southern horizon. He thought — It is as if birds, or helicopters, were after them.

He took the strap of the sub-machine gun down from his shoulder.

The soldier to whom the man who had first run over the horizon had been talking was looking at David Kahn; he seemed to make some gesture — a shrug, or a beckon, David Kahn couldn't tell — then he moved off with the man, and with other tourists, towards the southern bastion.

David Kahn thought — What would I have done in the time of Josephus?

Then — But does one not find oneself hypnotised, swept away, when there is drama, the threat of excitement?

When he reached the brow of the slope he could see people gathered along the railings of the southern bastion looking down into the ravine as if someone had fallen there. Another of his soldiers was running to the right where there was building equipment — pulleys and ropes — for raising stones. David Kahn thought — The top of this mountain is like a stage-set; step off it, and you would find yourself in a different world. To his left was the opening into the huge underground cistern in which, it had been suggested, the five children and two women who had survived the massacre at Masada had been hiding. This part of the story had always intrigued him: what had these seven done, how had they chosen, or been chosen, to survive? Other people did not seem much interested in this: they were more interested in the excitement and the killing. The soldier who had gestured to him was now coming towards him. David Kahn thought — But all this is happening very slowly; it is as if you had time, as with a painting, to let your eyes run over it. Then — But what was that myth I was told in my childhood about the seven just men? how there are seven Jews in any generation who, by their knowing and liveliness, keep the world going? He tested the action of his sub-machine gun. He thought — But what is knowing? what is liveliness? It is much easier, more dramatic, to want to die. The soldier said 'There are climbers.' David Kahn said 'Climbers.' The soldier said 'We're getting a rope.' He ran off back towards the southern bastion. David Kahn followed. He thought — But are they our climbers or theirs? are we trying to help them in or keep them out? Then — But what is ours or theirs if society is a whole? He came to the bottom of the steps that led up to the parapet of the southern bastion. To his left was another small opening in the vertical rock-face to the huge cistern in which the seven survivors at Masada were supposed to have hidden. He thought — But is it not just those who survive who keep the world going? He ran up the steps. He pushed his way through the crowd of tourists. Looking over the railings he saw the valley a thousand feet below. A short way down, as if clinging bodiless to the rock-face, was the upturned face of a young man. The soldier with David Kahn said 'There's another one below.' David Kahn said 'Another what?' The soldier said 'But he's dead. He's hanging on the end of the rope. He fell and hit his head.' Then — 'I think they're making a demonstration.' David Kahn, looking down, thought — But there's a painting like this: of the crucifixion: of the man's face, as seen from above, by God. He moved along the parapet; he saw that there was a rope going down from the waist of the man on the rock-face which was stretched tightly towards the valley below. He thought — And so, we destroy ourselves? He moved further to one side; he could not see past where the rope went down over a projection on the rock-face. He put a leg over the railings. The soldier said 'You can't go down.' One or two tourists said 'You can't go down without a rope.' David Kahn thought — But of course I must go down: it makes no difference if we are destroying ourselves. Then — I have to prove something to myself? If I want to stay alive? He said 'We can still save this one.' He was on the far side of the railings with his back to the drop below; he was trying to climb down the rock-face. He thought — I will climb down a little way and see if I can go no further: you do everything in due order, to survive. A tourist called — 'Stop him!' Another — 'You don't have to die!' David Kahn thought — Oh you believe that, do you? He was taking care to get good footholds and handholds as he climbed down. The first bit was not too steep: then there was the ledge to which the man with the upturned face was clinging. The man was now only a few yards away: he seemed to be hanging by his finger-tips. David Kahn said 'Can you hold on?' Then — 'I'll cut the rope.' The man had a fine beautiful face with a soft beard like Christ. His teeth were bared and he seemed to be screaming. David Kahn thought — But of course he won't want me to cut his rope: why is he here in the first place? David Kahn was trying to get out his knife. He thought — What is a demonstration, except that you are ready to die? Then — Life is a tightrope: but this is going the wrong way. He said 'I've got to cut the rope, your friend on the other end is dead, they saw him hit his head.' He got out his knife. He thought — but I've got to have one hand to hold on by and another to hold the rope and another to use the knife with. So I can't. Well, that's all right then. Then — But we should be able to get a rope going the right way? He looked up to the parapet where the second soldier was supposed to be bringing another rope: there were just the faces of tourists looking down. He thought — But it is now I who am a tadpole and God is looking down. Then — This is some new initiation? not circumcision? He turned back to the man on the rock-face: he stretched out his hand with the knife. The man spat at him. David Kahn thought — Well either one of you will die or both of you will. He said 'I tell you, the other one's dead.' With one hand he found an opening in the rock-face: he got a better hold. He thought — If I had more legs and arms: like Shiva! His hand with the knife in it just touched the rope. He thought — But what do these images mean: we are sperms clinging to a rock-face? Then the other man seemed to push himself off; he was on his back in the air for a moment; then he was rushing downwards as if through a trap-door into hell. David Kahn thought — But what I was trying to cut was an umbilical cord: not a foreskin; an umbilicus!

XVII

After Jason had first met Lilia he had stayed with her for two or three weeks: he had bought a toothbrush and shaving things and had moved into the small house in London she had been lent by friends. This was a time for both of them out of the normal run of their lives: the older man that Lilia had been living with was still abroad, and Jason had finished the script of a film for Epstien which was now being made in Rome. Lilia went out each day to a school of languages; Jason either stayed in the house and read, or went out to plays and films and art galleries. He thought — All right, this is a turning point; I must get out of films; I must find a new home; I must before it is too late write something that will try not just to describe things, but will alter them.

Lilia came home in the evenings with her books and home-work. He thought — We are both perhaps old enough now to be learning.

They did not talk much about their past lives. Jason told her about his children, who were now nearly grown up. The man whom Lilia had been living with would one day, they knew, come back from his lecture tour.

When they went to bed they clung on to each other and Jason thought — She is like a bear on a rock-face looking for honey.

— Or am I one of those wasps that plants its eggs in the paralysed bodies of caterpillars?

Then one day Lilia came back from her school and banged her books about as if they were bricks and mortar and she said 'Look, I'm serious.'

Jason said 'Up till now, you haven't been?'

She said 'You make everything a joke!'

He thought — The man she has been living with is coming back from Italy?

139

Then — She is pregnant?

— But there has not been time, surely, for her to know.

They went out to supper at a Pizza House. They sat at a table with a marble top and red iron legs. There was music from a juke box. Lilia said 'What are you going to do?'

He said 'You keep on talking as if one can choose.'

She said 'I chose you.'

She hacked away at her pizza.

Jason thought — I must try not to be clever.

The juke box poured out music like lava from a volcano. The pizzas were tough. Jason thought — Lava; larva; I would not know how to spell it.

She said 'Then what do you think will happen?'

He said 'I suppose we'll go off for a time, and then we'll find out if we want to come back to each other again.'

She said 'You want to go off?'

He said 'No, but I suppose I want to find out how much I'll want to come back.'

She pushed her plate away so violently that he had to catch a glass as it began to fall from the table.

He thought — This is one of the times when the earth flips: you either do or do not catch it.

When they were back in the house he lay on the bed and looked at the ceiling as he had done the night he first met her. He thought — I am like one of those effigies of dead crusaders.

She said 'Max is coming back tomorrow.'

He said 'Yes, I was getting ready for that.'

She said 'And I'll have to go back to our cottage in the country to join him.'

He thought — Max: Max: I must find out more about him.

She said 'So we must talk.'

He said 'I can't think of anything to say.'

He thought — Should I shout? break the furniture? go purple in the face, as they do in opera?

She said 'You had enough to say when you first loved me.'

He said 'You said that was all rubbish.'

When they were in bed he could feel her crying. She tried to cry quite silently, like an earthquake.

He said 'Look, of course you must go back. Of course I must go off and have a think somewhere. But of course it's awful if one says this.'

She said 'But you do care.'

'Yes I do care.'

'But you never sound as if you do.'

'If I sounded as if I did, I might not mean it.'

'Mightn't you?'

'No.'

'What do you feel then?'

'I think we're very lucky.'

'Lucky!'

He said 'We've had a good time.' He put his arms round her and held her.

He thought — She is like a tree with all her leaves being blown off.

Then — But the test will be, still, always, how much there is of rage and pain.

In the morning she packed and tidied the house as if she were punishing it. He thought — Because we have been happy here. As he watched her he thought — This strange creature with whom I have been sharing a burrow: what new monster will emerge?

He packed his own small bag. He put it by the front door where there was still on the table the postcard of Mary and Joseph and the infant Jesus going across the desert with their donkey.

He said 'Aren't you going to take this?'

She said 'If you loved me you'd try to stop me.'

He said 'I want to win.'

She said 'What do you want to win?'

He said 'Do you think a girl like you can be got by someone trying to stop you?'

He wondered — My eyes are blazing?

He thought for a moment she might come to him and kiss him and say something like — Oh I do love you! — and he did not think he could bear this, so he said —

'Shall we sing opera?'

She said 'Opera?'

He said 'You know, when they jump about and go purple in the face and try to stop each other.'

She sat down on her suitcase in the hall. She put her head in her hands. She seemed about to cry again.

He thought — She may not go?

Then he held out his arms and said '*Dammi il braccio mia piccina* — '

She looked up. She said 'What?'

He said 'Then they go out of that door.'

She said 'But Mimi died.'

He said 'But we're not going to die.'

She said 'Why not?'

He said 'Because we too can come alive again after the last act.'

He thought — She has not heard me say this before?

She said 'Oh I do love you!'

Then, when he was watching her drive away in a taxi, he thought — I am suffering pain already?

His wife from whom he was separated was away in California. His children were at boarding-school and university.

He thought — What I'm saying is, isn't it, that all the dramas, emotions, of our ordinary lives, are of little interest except insofar as we observe them, connect them, try to understand them, in order to make something quite different from them —

— To worry about them is cancer: to see the shape in them is life.

He went to Rome to see rushes of the film that was being made from a script of his by Epstien. He had a quarrel with Epstien about the way the script was being done. When the actors spoke their lines they acted in the old histrionic way as if they were trying to convince themselves that they had become the persons whom they were acting. Jason had written the script, he explained, to be spoken as if by people who knew they were actors.

Epstien said — For God's sake, I want it to be true!

Jason said — You think people who make themselves think they are other people are true?

While he was in Rome he was joined briefly by the girl he had been living with before he had met Lilia. He introduced her to Epstien. He knew Epstien would not like her. He thought — I am trying to kill two old birds with one stone?

His girlfriend said — You think Epstien is intelligent enough to know what truth is?

Epstien said — What is she, schizo?

Jason wondered — What is going on at that country cottage with its honeysuckle and roses —

— Max: Maximilian: are you like Julius Caesar, with laurel wreaths in your hair?

When he got back to London he was on his own again and he wondered if he should get in touch with Lilia. But he thought — I have got to believe in what I say; about waiting, watching, finding out; or how will I ever know what is true about this experiment?

One evening he was at a dinner party and a woman beside him said 'Max, you know, Max Ackerman: he's a biologist or physicist or something: I mean he's trying to do the two, which of course makes him unpopular: you know how academic people hate things being connected; he's interested in something like the way molecules work in the brain: I mean information, or patterning, or whatnot.'

And Jason thought — Ah, there are these connections which are true, which are to do with jealousy and pain!

The next day he went to a public library and looked up *Ackerman, Max* in an academic *Who's Who;* and he found that he was a professor at Cambridge, with an address in the country near by.

He thought — Is it any comfort to know that nothing grows and comes to fruition except through pain?

Then — Are you working on this, Max Ackerman, with your molecules in the brain?

He lay on his bed in a bed-sitting-room and thought — This is ridiculous.

— But I am not waiting for miracles: I have tried to work out, as a good scientist should, what are the probabilities of what I might want coming true.

One day Lilia rang him from the country. He thought — But of course, one still feels gratitude for what seems a miracle.

Lilia said 'Look, I must see you.'

He said 'Yes.'

She said 'Are you all right?'

He said 'No.'

She seemed to be waiting for him to say something more, so he said 'Where shall we meet?'

She came up to London and they sat either side of the unlit stove again in the house that had been lent to her by friends. She held a cigarette and backed away from it as if the smoke were coming after her. She said 'Look, it's really just to tell you that I can't see you again.'

He thought — But we are, and have not been, seeing each other again.

Then — So is that all right?

— Or shouldn't she be more clever?

He said 'Why not?'

She said 'Why does it matter?'

He thought — This is the sort of way I wanted my actors to act my film: as if they knew something quite different was going on.

She said 'I must make something of my life: I can't go on like this.'

He said 'I didn't think we had been going on.'

She said, as if she were hopeless, 'Haven't we?'

He wondered again — Is she pregnant?

He said 'Have you left Max? Has he left you?'

She said 'No.'

He said 'Well then.'

She puffed at her cigarette. He thought — She is like some balloon trying to take off across a channel.

She said 'And how about you?'

He said 'I've been in Rome. I travelled up through Italy. I missed you.'

She said 'And that's all.'

He said 'Dear God, what's all?'

He thought — Why do women so often behave in the way

144

men imagine they behave: is it something to do with the molecules in the brain?

He said 'Are you pregnant?'

She said 'Why do you say that?'

He said 'Because it's — what? — just over three months since I saw you.'

She said 'God damn, I do hate it when you're so smug!'

She seemed to be smiling.

Then she said 'I thought of getting rid of it.'

He thought — What if at last I get angry with her?

He said 'And what happened?'

She said 'Something stopped me.'

He said 'What stopped you?'

She said nothing.

He thought — It is she who is now manipulating this? to see what will happen?

Then — She has been talking to someone? Who? Not Max?

Then — Why do I think this?

She said 'I'm going to settle down with Max.'

He thought — No you're not.

He said 'Why are you telling me this now?'

She said 'I thought you might like to know.'

He thought — She thinks it will make things work if I hit her?

He said 'And now I know.'

He thought — Dear God, this balloon is coming back with fire and brimstone —

She said 'Why are you being so foul.'

He said 'I'm being foul!'

She said 'I hate you.'

He thought — I suppose we could settle down in some provincial town or somewhere.

He said 'Whose is the baby?'

She said 'I wouldn't marry you if you begged me!'

He thought — You wouldn't do anything if anyone begged you.

He said 'Is it mine? Is it his?' Then — 'Does he think it's his?'

She said 'Yes I think he thinks it's his.'

He said 'Well, you've got what you wanted, haven't you.'

He thought — And all that stuff about lighting candles at Assisi!

She seemed to be looking round for something to stub out her cigarette on, which would be like eyes.

He said 'Well you'd better settle down with me.'

She said 'Never!'

He said 'You come up here just to tell me that you'll never see me again: that you're going to have my baby — '

She said 'I haven't said it's your baby!'

He said ' — and that you're going to settle down with some-one else, just to hurt me, well you have hurt me — '

She glared at him, smiling.

He said 'You bitch.'

She picked up an ornament and threw it at him. It hit him on the shoulder.

He thought — But it was of iron!

He learned forwards and hit her with the back of his hand, not hard, across the face.

She put her head in her hands. She said 'You mustn't hurt me because of the baby.'

He said 'You should have thought of that before.'

She said 'I wanted you to feel something.'

He said 'And now I do.'

He thought — But what did she mean, she thought of getting rid of it but something stopped her?

She sat up and straightened her clothes. She was still smiling. She said 'But I couldn't have trapped you with the baby.'

He thought — No, because I knew.

He said 'Well we've trapped each other anyway.' Then — 'But how do I know it's my baby?'

She said 'Oh, but you do!'

XVIII

In the first-class compartment of the aeroplane Epstien was in the middle row on the left, Spud in the front row on the left, Wolf Tanner and Lisa Grant in the front on the right, the child and Jane in the middle on the right, Lilia and Jason at the back on the right, and the man called Julius across the aisle from Lilia in the back row on the left. Over the loudspeakers the passengers had been asked to fasten their seat-belts because of what the captain had called turbulence. Wolf Tanner had said 'Turbulence à la bonne femme.' Lilia had thought — We are those people staring at the wall of a cave: the shadows are what have followed us up from our unconscious?

Jason thought — Now the grubs from that paralysed caterpillar may break out and feed.

Epstien had put his oxygen mask away and now he leaned across the aisle to Wolf Tanner and said, as if it were a line from a straight man being fed to a comic — 'What was it Julius did to those two hankies in Rome, Wolf?'

Jason thought — They call them hankies, do they?

Wolf Tanner sang ' — Roolled them oover in the hoover — '

Lisa Grant said 'We're going to have to put you back in your pram, Epstien.'

Wolf Tanner sang ' — Foold them oover iron them out and do it again.'

Lilia thought — What was it Jason used to say: Shall we sing opera?

Jason thought — Oh that brave summer four years ago: what have I done since then? I have written, yes, what I wanted to write: which is to say that words are so often used like battering rams or defenceworks —

Epstien was saying 'How long do they keep in a laundry basket?'

Spud said 'About three days.'

Lisa Grant said 'I would have thought they would have smelt.'

Lilia was thinking — I used to ask him why he wrote it like that: he said — Because then you can know about shadows, and turn and protect yourself —

Jason thought — But still, how can one stay out of these caves, or cells?

Lilia was thinking — But how can you protect yourself, in the mind, against the people who in real life want to hurt you?

The man called Julius leaned across the aisle and said 'Hullo.'

Lilia said 'Hullo.'

Julius said 'Can I be introduced?' He was looking past her towards Jason.

Jason thought — There is some old cardboard dragon here with music coming out of his nostrils and eyebrows.

Lilia thought — But you did say, didn't you, Jason, that we had to go through rings of fire —

Julius called out — 'Hey, Wolf, this is the girl I was telling you about!'

Lilia said 'I must pee.'

Julius said 'I'll come too.'

Epstien said 'Do I owe you any money, Julius?'

Lilia unfastened her seat-belt and began to stand up. Jason put a hand out to stop her.

Jason thought — But we know about evil: you just have to turn your back on it, fart —

Lilia had thought — But I cannot bear this.

Jason thought — Then out of these old dragons' teeth some new life in the sun will grow.

A hostess came up and said 'Will you keep your seat-belts fastened please: there is some turbulence.'

Wolf Tanner said 'Turbulenzio alla Romana.'

Lilia looked for her child. The child was sitting with the girl called Jane in the seats in front.

Lilia thought — In what way could the plane crash and every-one be killed except Jason and me and the child? — and, all right, Jane, because she is being nice to my child.

Epstien said 'Hey, Julius! If you had them strapped to their seats, you could really show them some stuff!'

Lisa Grant said 'What is a stuff movie?'

Spud said 'It's not stuff it's snuff.'

Wolf Tanner said 'Stuff is enough.'

Spud said 'It's when someone actually dies.'

Then he looked back at Jason.

Jason thought — What on earth is going on? Spud is really the man who thought he'd shot me in that war, but hadn't?

Then — It's because of their ugliness, these people will die?

Wolf Tanner had also been leaning round into the aisle. He seemed to be trying to speak to Lilia, or to Jason.

He said 'It's cheaper to cheat.'

Epstien said 'At five hundred dollars a seat?'

Lilia said to Epstien 'What are you afraid of — women?'

Jason thought — Oh these girls! it's they who come out fighting like Siegfried now! Will they win, if they don't get sidetracked by falling in love with women?

Epstien said to Lilia 'Did he have his ring on?'

Jason thought — His ring?

Wolf Tanner said 'Oh my faithless piggywig!' Then he turned to his front and stared at the wall.

Lilia said 'Do you have to have a ring to get yourselves up by?'

Jason began laughing. He thought — Oh all right! but then men will have to become stage-managers instead of Brünnhildes, so that there will be someone left alive at the end of the last act —

He said 'Let me sit there.'

Lilia said 'No I'm all right.'

He stood up and began to squeeze past Lilia. Lilia moved to the window seat where he had been. Jason sat by the aisle. He was now next to the man called Julius in the seat on the other side of the aisle. The hostess said 'Will you keep your seat-belts fastened please.'

Jason said to Jane 'Can you hand him over?'

Jane said 'Yes.' She helped the child over the top of the seat in front of Jason.

Lilia said 'What are you doing?'

Jason said to the child 'Now who exactly is this awful man as has got sweeties?'

His child looked at him. Then he looked at Julius, then at Epstien, then at Wolf Tanner.

Epstien looked away.

The child said 'The man as has got sweeties in his bag.'

Jason said 'What sort of sweeties? What sort of bag?'

Lilia said about her child 'You can't use him!'

Jason said 'Why not?'

The child said 'Little white sweeties like ballies.'

Jason said 'Little white ballies.'

The child said 'Yes.'

Jason said 'Little white ballies like maggots.'

Everyone had stopped laughing.

Jason wondered if he should explain to Lilia — You think we can't win? Children are part of us —

The man called Julius took a box out of his pocket and held it out to Jason and the child. It contained what looked like small white pills. He said 'Here.'

Lilia leaned across Jason and seemed to make a grab for the pills. Jason, leaning back, kicked at the underneath of the man's hand and the box flew out of it and pills were scattered on the floor.

Jason thought — Now why did I do that?

Julius went down on his hands and knees on the floor after the pills. He found one, looked up at Lilia belligerently, and put the pill in his mouth.

Spud left his seat and came down the aisle and stood over Julius. He picked up the box of pills and looked at it and put it in his pocket. Then he took hold of Julius by the hair and pulled his head up and slapped him on the side of the face. Then he looked at Jason.

Jason thought — This is all to do with something going on, or having once gone on, elsewhere?

Julius put a hand up to his cheek.

Then Wolf Tanner got up, came down the aisle and stood over Julius. He said 'Who's been eating *my* pudding.' He mimed aiming a kick at Julius. Julius, staring up at Wolf Tanner belligerently, put a finger inside his mouth and swallowed.

Jason thought — They are not play-acting?

The hostess was saying 'Will you keep your seat-belts fastened please, or I'll have to call the captain.'

Spud seemed to be picking pills up from the floor. Then he went back to his seat.

Wolf Tanner said 'And don't worry if he starts groaning and rolling about.' Then he went back to his seat.

Jason thought — They are like players who have done what they have to do in a game of hunt-the-thimble.

Lisa Grant, trying to look back over the top of her seat, said 'It's like watching executions in the eighteenth century.'

Spud said 'It's not like watching executions in the eighteenth century.'

Epstien was staring to his front as if there were shadows on the wall.

Julius had crawled up sideways onto the two seats on the left at the back and had lain down on his front.

Jason thought — It was always just that he was on drugs?

Lilia was thinking — But he didn't give my child one of those pills, did he? He didn't give Jason one of those pills?

She said 'He didn't give him one of those pills, did he?'

Jason said 'No.'

Lilia said to her child 'You didn't take one of those pills, did you?'

Jason thought — But dear God, still, what was it that was going on in the lavatory?

Jane, looking over the top of the row of seats in front, said 'Jason — '

He said 'Yes?'

She said 'Those people, you know, that you seem to be writing about, who thought they knew something they had to keep secret, in the first century — '

Jason thought — Dear God, is she trying to tell me something in code?

He said 'Yes?'

She said 'What were they called?'

He said 'Gnostics.'

She said 'And what was it they thought they knew?'

He said 'They thought they knew God, which was the way things worked. But this was a different God from the one other people thought they knew, so they had to keep it secret, to stay alive.'

Jane said 'And so that it could stay alive — '

Jason said 'Yes.'

He thought — This is the code?

Lilia was thinking — I can go on saying, can't I, that that man asked me to help him, so I said Yes: and we went along to the lavatory and he asked me to give him an injection, but I said No. I don't know why he asked me, but I have been trained as a nurse —

The steward, with the hostess, was trying to get Julius to move his legs which were sticking out into the aisle.

Lilia was thinking — I can go on saying, can't I, that he asked me to help him —

The hostess said 'Is he on something?'

Spud said 'He's on things like angels are on the points of needles.'

Jason thought — Well, that's witty.

Lisa Grant said 'This really is a snuff movie!'

The plane gave a lurch. Lilia held on to the sides of her seat. She said 'Should we be frightened?'

Jason said 'No.'

Then their child, who was sitting on Jason's knee, said 'My don't want to be borned again!'

Spud and Epstien had been looking at each other. Then Spud raised his arms as if he were surrendering. Then Epstien looked at Jason.

Jason was saying to his child 'Why don't you want to be borned again?'

His child said 'Men come after me with knives! Men hit me!'

Jason said 'They hit you? Where did they hit you?'

His child put a hand against his stomach.

The hostess was going up towards the captain's cabin.

The legs of Julius, lying on his front, were kicking out into the aisle.

Jason said to Lilia 'Did you hear that?'

Lilia said 'Yes.'

Jason said to his child 'You remember when you were borned?'

His child said 'They pushed a trunk down my mouth — '

Jason said 'A trunk — '

His child said 'Of an elephant.'

He opened his mouth and pointed a finger inside.

Jason thought — Dear God, it's true the nurse did seem to be rough with him —

Julius' legs kept kicking out into the aisle.

Jane, from the seat in front, said 'That is an extraordinary child!'

The child said 'They put sticks up my nose!'

Jason said 'Sticks up your nose?'

Lilia said 'It's all right!'

The child said 'And stop my arms — '

Jason said 'But your arms are all right! look! look! and your nose! your mouth! your tummy!'

His child said 'My don't want to be borned again!'

Jason said 'You're not going to be borned again! You're all right! Now! You're wonderful!'

Lilia said 'Look! here's Mummy! Daddy!'

The steward was saying 'We must wait for the captain.'

Spud was saying 'Does anyone know where we're going yet?'

Lilia was thinking — There are always violences, deaths, at a nativity?

XIX

SCENE: Masada 73 A.D. The southern bastion.

Philomela and the Old Woman from Jotapata are on the battlements.

Philomela walks up and down. The Old Woman sits with her back against a wall.

Philomela acts as if narrating someone else's speech —

> PHILOMELA
>
> — My loyal followers, long ago we resolved to serve neither the Romans nor anyone else but only God, who alone is the true and righteous Lord of men: now the time has come that bids us prove our determination by our deeds —

She glances into the camera.

Then she looks away across the plateau.

She says in her ordinary voice —

> PHILOMELA
>
> Or that sort of thing. You know. With his heart in his hands. Our Eleazar! They didn't like it much at first. But you get them in the end. With the death bit.

She acts again as if narrating Eleazar's speech —

> PHILOMELA
>
> — Ever since primitive man began to think, the words of our ancestors and of the gods, supported by the actions and spirit of our forefathers, have constantly impressed on us that life is the calamity for man, not death. Death gives freedom to our souls and lets them depart to their own pure home where they will know nothing of any calamity; but while they are confined within a mortal body and share its miseries, in strict truth they are dead. For association of the divine with the mortal is most improper —

154

Then she says in her ordinary voice —

PHILOMELA

Getting fucked by God is most improper.

So watch out, children! —

Your daddies are coming after you with knives —

She looks down over the parapet towards the opening into the underground cistern.

PHILOMELA

You know *Medea*?

We used to play it in Jerusalem.

They loved it.

She walks up and down on the parapet. She acts —

PHILOMELA

— For they must die, and since they must then I who gave them birth must kill them. Arm yourself, my heart! The thing that you must do is fearful yet inevitable —

OLD WOMAN

You told them that?

PHILOMELA

And then she kills her children.

To get her own back. On their father.

She looks across the plateau of Masada.

OLD WOMAN

And they believed you?

PHILOMELA

Oh they always do, you know. People.

If you do it well enough.

It's called suspension of disbelief —

OLD WOMAN

What a dreadful phrase.

PHILOMELA

Yes isn't it.

She walks up and down. She acts Eleazar's speech again —

PHILOMELA

— Let our wives die unabused, our children without knowledge of slavery; after that, let us do each other an ungrudging kindness, preserving our freedom as a glorious winding-sheet —

Then she says in her ordinary voice —
> PHILOMELA
> He really did say that.
> You wouldn't believe it.
> Christ!
> I think they feel it as a sort of bell.
> Their mother's heart-beat.

She acts —
> PHILOMELA
> — These things are God's vengeance for the many wrongs that in our madness we dared do to our own countrymen —

She says in her ordinary voice —
> PHILOMELA
> That was a bit they didn't like.

She acts in a comic voice —
> PHILOMELA
> — Me, in my state of health? —

Then she leans over the parapet and calls —
> PHILOMELA
> So watch out children, your daddies are going to make an imperishable art-work of you, with knives!

She glances into the camera.

Then she walks up and down. She acts —
> PHILOMELA
> — But even if from the very first we had been taught some contrary belief, that life is indeed the greatest good of mankind and death a disaster, the situation is such that we should still be called on to bear death with a stout heart; for God's will and sheer necessity doom us to it —

She says in her ordinary voice —
> PHILOMELA
> Absolutely true.
> I think it's the boredom of their own voice that gets them.
> — If you don't eat it up for dinner you'll get it back for tea —

With knives. With knobs on.

She acts —

> PHILOMELA

— So let us deny the enemy their hoped-for pleasure at
our expense, and without more ado leave them to be
dumbfounded by our death and awed by our courage —

She appears exhausted. She says in her ordinary voice —

> PHILOMELA

I'm deader than you.

Yah boo. Sucks.

Our mother's heart-beat.

> OLD WOMAN

You said you'd kill them? The children?

> PHILOMELA

It's all in the mind —

She acts —

> PHILOMELA

— Take now thy son, thine only son Isaac, whom thou
lovest, and offer him for a burnt offering upon one of
the mountains I will tell thee of —

> OLD WOMAN

But Abraham didn't —

> PHILOMELA

But they think he would have done.

And twice on Saturdays.

She acts —

> PHILOMELA

— Lady! Lady! Lady! Alas! Alas!

Help! Help! My Lady's dead! —

> OLD WOMAN

Where did you get that?

> PHILOMELA

It came into my mind.

A wave —

A heart-beat.

She glances into the camera.

Then she walks up and down.

PHILOMELA

Hullo, hullo, can you hear me?

— Become as wise as serpents and as innocent as doves —

OLD WOMAN

He said that?

PHILOMELA

Him. Who. That other one.

She seems to quote —

PHILOMELA

— And when you make the two one, and the inner as the outer, and the outer as the inner, and the above as the below, and when you make the male and the female into a single one —

She stares across the plateau of Masada.

After a time —

OLD WOMAN

Yes?

PHILOMELA

— Whoever finds the explanation of these words will not taste death —

OLD WOMAN

You said it as if you believed it.

PHILOMELA

And so can it or can't it be true —

He both did and didn't die —

Or — What I'm trying to do is to protect them?

She looks down over the parapet.

PHILOMELA

What else did he say?

Him. Who. That single one.

OLD WOMAN

Trust. God is inside you.

Philomela faces out over the plateau again. She acts —

PHILOMELA

— But even if from the very first we had been taught some contrary belief —

She stops.

PHILOMELA

And so on. And so on.

OLD WOMAN

They believe we'd kill the children?

PHILOMELA

It goes round and round.

Like a sieve.

A riddle.

OLD WOMAN

And what's left —

PHILOMELA

Survives.

She looks down over the parapet.

PHILOMELA

Why do they cut their penises, do you know?

OLD WOMAN

Oh I think it's to do with making them one of a tribe.

PHILOMELA

And what is trusting?

OLD WOMAN

I think it's to do with knowing you're one of the tribe.

PHILOMELA

And that's the difference —

OLD WOMAN

Yes.

Philomela walks up and down again. She seems to quote —

PHILOMELA

— Two will rest on a bed: the one will die, the one will live —

OLD WOMAN

But that depends where you begin —

PHILOMELA

Well, where did we?

OLD WOMAN

What will you do when the Romans come?

PHILOMELA

That sounds like the title to a song.

She looks out over the plateau. Then she acts —

PHILOMELA

— Hullo, hullo, can you hear me? —

There is a scream from the far side of the plateau.
The women listen.

PHILOMELA

I think it's a matter of language —
Language finds it easy to say what things are not:
not to say what things are.

There are more screams from across the plateau.
The women listen.

PHILOMELA

They've started the killing. They're killing their children.

OLD WOMAN

I think it's something to do with when they are borned.

PHILOMELA

Borned!

OLD WOMAN

People come after them with sticks, and knives —

They listen.

There are more screams from across the plateau.

PHILOMELA

Bedtime stories, children.
— I am alive, you are dead —
— Mummy. Mummy —

OLD WOMAN

And so, when the Romans come —

Philomela acts —

PHILOMELA

— Hullo, my good man, will you take me to your
leader —

OLD WOMAN

It's a sort of style —

Philomela looks round as if she had suddenly noticed they
are on a film set.

PHILOMELA

— I say, what is this place? —

OLD WOMAN

What do you mean, what is this place?

160

PHILOMELA

— What do you mean what do I mean —

She looks over the parapet.

PHILOMELA

— It's only two foot to the bottom!

She glances into the camera.

They listen.

There is silence from across the plateau.

OLD WOMAN

Go on —

PHILOMELA

What —

It happens off-stage?

They've done it.

They think we've done it?

The old woman seems to rehearse Philomela.

OLD WOMAN

— Hullo hullo, my good man —

PHILOMELA

— I have a message for your leader —

OLD WOMAN

— Oh, and what is your message? —

PHILOMELA

— These children are immortal —

OLD WOMAN

— Oh why are they immortal? —

PHILOMELA

— Because they have survived —

OLD WOMAN

— And why have they survived? —

PHILOMELA

— Because they are immortal —

OLD WOMAN

— And why are they immortal? —

She looks down over the parapet. Then she looks out across the plateau. She seems to have stopped acting.

OLD WOMAN

You think they'll accept it?

PHILOMELA

Oh, they'll accept anything.

That survives.

She looks out across the plateau.

PHILOMELA

It's called affirming the consequent.

Survival of the fittest.

OLD WOMAN

What dreadful phrases!

PHILOMELA

Yes aren't they.

So don't tell anyone.

OLD WOMAN

You think we're telling anyone!

From across the plateau there is the sound of falling masonry.

PHILOMELA

— And then a little bird flew down! —

OLD WOMAN

I thought it was tongues of fire.

They listen.

After a time —

PHILOMELA

— Hullo hullo, my good man, I have a message for —

OLD WOMAN

— Your reader?

PHILOMELA

— Leader!

Philomela, acting, leans against the parapet of the southern bastion.

A section of the parapet breaks. Philomela nearly falls over.

She recovers. She holds a section of the parapet. It appears to be made of plywood.

She looks at it. She recites —

PHILOMELA

— Now the serpent was more subtle than any beast of the field —

She looks into the camera. She smiles.

XX

Deborah Kahn was a security officer at Lod airport near Tel Aviv. Her job was to interview passengers after their luggage had been searched and they had been through emigration control, and before they went to the departure lounges where they passed through metal-detector and X-ray machines and where their clothes and hand-luggage were searched again. It was Deborah Kahn's job to ask the passengers questions about where they came from, where they were going, what they had been doing in Israel, whom they had seen; had anyone been in a position to put anything in their luggage without their knowledge, and so on. Deborah Kahn carried out these interviews in one of a row of small cubicles like changing-rooms which had a door at each end and a bench along one side and a counter on the other. If she thought there was anything suspicious about a passenger she could send him or her for further questioning to a guard room at the end of the row of cubicles. The cubicles were open at the top, so that what was going on inside could be kept under observation from platforms and from closed-circuit television under the roof.

Deborah Kahn had learned that what she was doing in her job was partly to listen to the content of what people told her but also to be listening for something she could not quite name but which seemed to be to do with the style, the pattern, the type of answering that people gave to her: something to do with whether or not, or in what way, people were acting — or were trying to act as though they were not acting — this raising the whole question of what acting was and what it was not. She had come to notice something peculiar here: which was that it was the people who appeared in some self-evident way to be acting — those who answered her questions jovially, disarmingly, nervously or even apparently guiltily — who were in a

practical way most probably harmless, in that they were unlikely to be the sort of people who would cause a disturbance
or blow up a plane; and it was those people (she had not come
across many who were like this yet: this was mainly an impression she had got from people who were the opposite) who
might appear to be completely sincere and all-of-a-piece who,
just because of this, might be slightly mad and therefore
dangerous. She had had two or three such cases — men and
women who had come into her cubicle and who had appeared
such rounded, purposive characters that they had seemed to
her like puppets: she had sent them for further questioning. In
two cases it had been found that they were carrying drugs, and
in the third case a 'woman' had turned out to be a man. In this
latter case, what had made Deborah Kahn suspicious was just
that the person had appeared so essentially and dramatically a
woman that this had not seemed true.

Deborah Kahn had discussed this with her husband David,
who was doing his military service at Masada. He had said 'You
mean, if someone seems to believe in himself too simply, he is
not quite human?'

She had said 'People, like things, in fact are always changing.'

He had said 'I don't know how this fits in with being ready to
die for one's beliefs.'

She had thought — He is worrying about those people at
Masada?

She had said 'I think one could be ready to die, and still be
choosing to live.'

He had said 'You mean, one would be choosing to know one
was always changing?'

Deborah Kahn was a student of physics; David, of psychology.

They used to have such conversations between themselves:
they had not found many other people to have them with in
Israel.

Then one day there came into Deborah's cubicle a girl of such
obvious and intense nervousness that she seemed deliberately
to be acting: Deborah Kahn for once felt almost frightened: she
thought — This girl must be doing it for some purpose: she is
only pretending to be like someone on drugs or smuggling or

intending to blow up a plane: does she think people will then not believe she can be? and so we will let her through? The girl had short black hair and a brown face with no make-up. She wore an anorak and jeans and carried a rucksack. She frowned at Deborah Kahn intently as if she were hoping to be recognised: or as if she were wondering whether she were getting through some message. Deborah Kahn thought — I have known her in another world? she is like myself?

She asked the girl the usual questions. The girl said she was an actress and came from Canada. She had been with a troupe of travelling puppet-players touring Israel.

Deborah Kahn thought — She is acting in such a way that it is as if she expects me to know who she really is, but does not want me to acknowledge this?

She said 'Can you empty out your bag please.'

The girl said 'No.'

Deborah Kahn said 'I must ask — '

The girl smiled and put her rucksack down on the counter.

Then she looked up to the ceiling of the airport building as if she realised that there would be people and cameras watching there.

Deborah Kahn thought — She is using some code?

Then — She has got the wrong person?

The girl unfastened her rucksack and held the top open.

Deborah Kahn thought — Or I am being made her accomplice?

Then the girl said 'Have you got it?'

Deborah Kahn leaned with her back against the counter where there was, under the ledge at the far end, an alarm switch which could summon help to her.

Then she thought — But if she thinks I am another person, an accomplice, should I not find out more about this?

— I will not be doing my duty if I just press the alarm switch?

— Or I am just being taken in by her?

She said 'Got what — '

The girl said 'The gun.'

Then she put her head back and made a face as if she were laughing.

Deborah Kahn thought — She is mad.

— Or she is just joking?

The girl said 'You don't remember me.'

Deborah Kahn said 'No.'

The girl said 'Sorry.' She pulled her rucksack towards her and fastened the top.

Deborah Kahn thought — This way people can send other people mad: because you do not know not just whether or not you are being taken in, but what being taken in is.

She said 'I must ask you again — '

Then the girl looked round the walls of the cubicle as if she were afraid. She said 'You won't hurt me?'

Deborah Kahn thought — But if all this is an act —

— And she wants me to press the alarm switch so as to create a diversion —

The girl seemed to stand to attention and said 'Yes, I've been with this touring company. We've been playing to schools.'

She said this loudly. Then she opened her rucksack again. She put her hand inside.

She said 'Keep talking.'

Deborah Kahn thought — She has got a gun?

Then — But if she wants to create a diversion still I should do nothing?

Deborah Kahn said 'Look, you won't get away with this.'

She thought — But this is ridiculous!

The girl said 'Yes, we've been doing a modern version of *Antigone* and *The Caucasian Chalk Circle* — '

She was looking up at the roof of the airport building.

Deborah Kahn thought — If she pulls a gun out now people from under the roof will simply shoot her.

— So should I not stop them?

The girl said 'Of course I haven't got a gun!' She smiled.

Deborah Kahn said 'Empty that bag.'

The girl said 'You don't know what to do, do you.'

Deborah Kahn thought — She goes in and out of frames like a —

— Atom — ?

— Particle — ?

— Wave — ?

Then — I am being hypnotised?

She said again 'Empty that bag.'

The girl said 'Look!' She took out of her bag something that looked like a hand-grenade. Then she screwed it up in her hand and laid it on the counter where it seemed to be a lump of plasticine.

The girl said 'One, two, three, four — '

Then she put her head back and laughed again.

Deborah Kahn thought — Well, they didn't shoot her.

The girl said 'You don't know what to believe!'

Deborah Kahn thought — She is one of those people making some demonstration?

The girl seemed to stand to attention again. She said 'I'm a member of an organisation — '

Then she crouched and put her hands over her ears.

Deborah Kahn thought — Well, they will shoot her.

She said 'Why are you doing this?'

The girl straightened and took her hands away from her ears. Then she picked up the lump of plasticine and held it to her mouth as if it were a microphone. She said 'Testing, testing — '

Deborah Kahn thought — She is a member of some security control group come to test me?

She said 'This is what you do?'

The girl put the lump of plasticine back on the counter. She said 'What?'

Deborah Kahn said 'I'm trying to help you.'

The girl said 'Yes. I told you. I'm an actress in a puppet theatre. We control puppets.' She said this loudly.

Deborah Kahn thought — I don't want her shot because —

She said 'What do you control?'

The girl said 'You. The people in the control-tower.'

Then she looked up again to the roof of the airport building.

Deborah Kahn thought — Afterwards, I can make out I knew what was going on all the time.

She said 'No one's going to hurt you.'

The girl said 'They're watching?'

Deborah Kahn said 'Yes.'

The girl said 'I just want you to know how silly I think all this is.'

Deborah Kahn said 'What is silly?'

The girl said 'Your play-acting. Don't you think? Have you got incurable cancer?'

Then she put her hand in her rucksack and took out what looked like a real grenade. She held it in one hand and put a finger of her other hand through the ring.

She said 'It's a toy for my child! It's made of plasticine!'

Deborah Kahn said 'They'll shoot you.'

The girl said 'Have I been here four minutes?'

Deborah Kahn thought — I should now press the alarm switch.

There was the sound of machine-gun fire from somewhere outside. The walls of the cubicle seemed to go in and out slightly. Then the door burst open and a man in camouflage uniform came in and shot the girl twice in the head with a pistol that did not make much noise. The girl moved as if a car had hit her. There had been a look on her face —

The man in uniform tried to catch the grenade as it fell to the floor.

There had been a look on her face —

The man in uniform put an arm round Deborah Kahn and rushed her out of the cubicle and across a space which seemed to have been cleared of people and pushed her down behind one of the emigration desks and lay with his hands over his head and an arm over her own.

A look on her face —

Deborah Kahn wanted to say — But she was only trying to tell us this was silly!

After a time she said 'You needn't have killed her.'

She tried to get up. The man pulled her down.

Deborah Kahn said 'It was a toy.'

She got up and started walking back towards the cubicle. The space that had been cleared was like the surface of the moon. The man in uniform followed her. He said 'You did all right!'

Deborah Kahn thought — Oh yes, that will be the story.

She said 'Was anyone else involved?'

He said 'Yes, two men on the runway.'

Inside the cubicle the girl was lying with her face against the wall. The side of her head seemed to have gone. The man picked up the grenade which was lying on the ground. It appeared to be a real one, but empty.

Deborah Kahn said 'Who were they?'

The man said 'We don't know.'

He was emptying the contents of the girl's rucksack on to the counter. It contained a few clothes, and a child's teddy-bear.

The man in uniform hit the stomach of the teddy-bear with the butt of his sub-machine gun. It made a mewing noise.

Deborah Kahn said 'I think she was making some kind of protest.'

The man said 'What kind of protest?'

Deborah Kahn said 'It's difficult to say.'

She thought — The look on her face was like that of a mother watching her child come home from war.

XXI

Lisa Grant said 'That man's dead.'

Spud said 'He's sleeping.'

Wolf Tanner said 'On a dark night, you can tell the difference?'

Epstien, in the middle row on the left, had his eyes closed and held his oxygen mask on his lap. Julius was sprawled over the seats on the left at the back.

The steward, still trying to lift Julius' feet out of the aisle, said 'Doesn't anyone know what he's been taking?'

Spud said 'It looked like commodores.'

Wolf Tanner said 'You call that commodores?'

Lisa Grant said 'This really is a snuff movie!'

The hostess had come down the aisle with the captain. The captain was a grey-haired man who held his cap under his arm like a helmet. They stood looking down at the body of Julius.

Jason thought — The captain is like the Roman general on Masada?

The captain said 'Don't any of you know him?'

The hostess looked at Lilia.

Lilia was sitting by the window next to Jason with their child on her lap.

Spud said 'He came up here — '

Lisa Grant said 'I don't know him.'

Wolf Tanner said 'Not in the unbiblical sense.'

The captain and the steward stared at Wolf Tanner and Lisa Grant.

Lilia was thinking — He asked me to go with him to the lavatory: he wanted me to give him an injection: I have been a nurse —

The captain said 'This man is in some trouble.'

The hostess said 'I think he's dead.'

The steward had turned Julius over on to his back and had opened his anorak and shirt. He crawled on top of him as if he were assaulting him.

Lilia thought — But I wanted him dead?

The hostess drew the curtain at the back of the first-class compartment. Then she felt in Julius' pockets.

Then she said to Lilia 'You were with him?'

Lilia said 'Yes.'

The captain stared at her.

Jason thought — The Romans have broken in. We have survived the suicide pact: now we have to deal with the Romans on Masada.

The steward had his mouth on Julius' mouth.

Lilia said 'He asked me if I could help him with an injection. He said something had gone wrong. I have been a nurse.'

Jason thought — Now look at the captain straight, but not too straight; not as if you were trying to put something over.

The hostess said 'They were in the lavatory.'

The captain said 'The lavatory.'

Lilia said 'I couldn't make any sense of him.'

Jason thought — Now say nothing more.

The captain said 'You gave him an injection?'

Lilia said 'No.'

The captain said 'But he wanted you to?'

Lilia said 'No.'

The captain and the hostess stared at her.

Jason thought — Dear God, Lilia, you can't take on all the evils of the world —

Jane, from the seat in the middle on the right, said 'Epstien, come down and help us.'

Epstien had not moved for some time. Jason had been thinking — God is pretending to be dead and living in the Argentine.

Jane said 'Wasn't he someone who used to follow us around?'

Spud said 'Oh yes, wasn't he?'

Lisa Grant said 'There are people like that — '

The captain transferred his cap from underneath one arm to underneath the other. The steward was banging on Julius' chest.

Jason thought — Come on, you actors, you're professionals —

Lilia said 'He showed me some pills. He said they'd been carried by the Nazi leaders in the last war.'

The captain said 'The Nazi leaders in the last war.'

The hostess held out the small box of pills. The captain poked at them gingerly.

Spud said 'These people do it for effect: it happens all the time.'

He turned round and stared at Jason.

Jason thought — All right, all right, we've got the message —

The steward had climbed off Julius. The captain took the box of pills and put it in his pocket. Then the steward handed to him a small square of paper, which he smelled.

The hostess said 'But what happened then?'

Lilia said 'What happened then?'

Jason thought — That's all!

Lilia said 'He was obviously in some sort of distress.'

Jason thought — You're not expected to say anything after 'distress'!

Then Epstien's huge moon face came round into the aisle. It seemed quite blank. He said 'These people follow us around. Yes. They cause enormous trouble.'

He stared at the captain.

Jason thought — The power of film people is that they, like gods, can hypnotise people, by some impression of immortality —

The captain said 'You're all in on this film business?'

He had moved away from Julius. He was speaking to Epstien.

Wolf Tanner said 'I'm not!'

Epstien said 'Oh yes you are.'

Wolf Tanner said 'Oh I thought you meant — ' He laughed.

Epstien said 'It's a film about Masada. You know about Masada? Where those patriots killed themselves.'

The captain said 'Brave chaps.'

Epstien said 'Yes.'

Jason thought — Epstien, you are clever!

Then — The hypnosis is, that the captain will not even know

what he is being taken in by.

Wolf Tanner began to sing ' — By the light of the silvery moon, the moon — '

Epstien said 'Wolf, will you come in on this please!'

Lilia was thinking — Wolf, as the boyfriend, is suffering?

Epstien said to the captain 'Yes, as a story it has everything.'

Jane thought — So as a story it tells nothing?

Lisa Grant said 'This *is The Petrified Forest.*'

Wolf Tanner looked round at Lilia.

Epstien was saying 'There are a lot of people involved in this film. A lot of prestige. It would be a tragedy to lose it. It's got government backing.'

Wolf Tanner said 'Would you good people care to join us in a drink?'

He was climbing out of his seat. In the aisle he hitched up his trousers. Then he turned and held a hand out to the hostess.

The hostess was staring at him as if entranced with her hands held close to her sides.

Lilia thought — Now do your smile that goes up higher on one side than the other —

Epstien was saying 'The point is, who would benefit if the film were prevented from being made?'

Spud said 'Yes who would benefit if the film were prevented from being made?'

The captain said 'You mean, this might be some plot?'

Wolf Tanner said 'A plot!' He put his hand on his heart. Then he said 'Some corner of a foreign field — '

The steward had moved across the aisle and was looking down at Lisa Grant, who was smiling up at him.

Spud said 'The thing is, we work to such tight deadlines.'

Epstien said 'God, these martyrs! How they can bitch people up!' He flung himself back in his seat.

Lilia thought — Would it help if his chair broke, and we could laugh?

The hostess was moving up the aisle towards Wolf Tanner.

The captain said 'But of course the film must be made!'

Epstien said 'We don't ask for anything improper: cover-up — '

Wolf Tanner was saying 'What does a pretty girl like you do in Casablanca?' He was making a gesture for the hostess to sit in one of the seats at the front on the left.

Lisa Grant was saying to the steward 'Have we got any more of that champagne?'

Jason thought — Now don't overdo it!

The captain was saying 'He just came up here from the tourist-class?'

Lilia was thinking — But of course I am responsible for the evils of the world —

— I stretched across for those pills: Jason knocked the box out of his hand: he knelt on the floor: the man called Spud came and hit him across the face: Wolf Tanner pretended to kick at him —

Jane was looking over the top of the seat in front and was saying to Jason 'We are being circumcised?'

Jason frowned and shook his head.

The hostess had sat down in a seat at the front on the left by Wolf Tanner. Wolf Tanner was saying 'Have you ever seen a film being made?'

Lisa Grant was saying 'Does anyone know where we're going?'

The steward was saying 'What about some brandy!'

Lilia was thinking — Then he seemed to put a pill in his mouth. Or he already had a pill in his mouth. He swallowed it. When the man hit him? Or he felt rejected by Wolf Tanner? He was on cocaine: heroin. It was an accident. He drank whisky —

— But why him?

— Why anyone?

— We are all in guilt like a seed-pod; from which some, but not others, emerge —

Spud was saying 'You've got his passport?'

The captain was saying 'I don't see why you people should be troubled by the authorities.' He had sat down in the seat opposite Epstien. Epstien was spreading across the aisle towards him like oil.

Lilia was clinging on to her child.

Her child said 'Mummy — '

She said 'Yes?'

Her child said 'Why are you crying?'

Jason said 'It's all right. It's all right.'

She said 'I know.'

She was thinking — That poor serpent, with everyone's foot on it!

Jason said 'We'll be coming down soon.'

Lilia thought — In some dreadful way I did quite like him.

The hostess was saying 'Have you been in a disaster movie?'

Wolf Tanner was saying 'I *am* a disaster movie.'

The steward was pouring brandy for Lisa Grant.

Spud said 'Have we got the lady's luggage up yet?' He was looking at Lilia.

Jane said 'Did you ever think the film could be made?' She was talking to Jason.

Jason said 'No.'

He thought — And you, with your grey-green eyes, I thought I might run hand in hand along some beach with you —

Epstien was saying 'I expect you get quite a bit of this sort of thing.'

The captain was saying 'Yes we do get quite a bit of this sort of thing.'

Jane said to Jason 'Do you want me to get back those scripts?'

Jason said 'No let them be scattered — '

The voice of the assistant pilot came over the loudspeakers asking the passengers to ensure their seat-belts were fastened and that their seats were in an upright position.

Wolf Tanner called out — 'I think the captain and his crew should have dinner with us!'

Lisa Grant called out — 'Yes I think the captain and his crew should have dinner with us!' She raised her glass.

The captain exclaimed — 'If you good people keep me here any longer we won't be anywhere for dinner!'

Epstien and Spud and Wolf Tanner and Lisa Grant laughed.

Then the captain got up and went back to his cabin.

The hostess and the steward moved back down the aisle.

Jason thought — And now when we all have those smiles on our faces like mad archaic statues —

— What is that scene where there are beautiful people walking on a beach; and beyond them, over the sand dunes, there is a temple where witches are dismembering a child?

The steward had fetched a blanket and was pulling it over Julius' face.

Jason thought — We will none of us quite talk about him being dead.

Lilia was holding on tightly to her child.

Jane said 'Does anyone know where in fact we're coming down?'

Spud said 'Yes, by the Red Sea.'

Jason thought he might once have said — You see, I told you!

Lilia would have said — You are a magician!

Wolf Tanner was looking over the top of his seat and was saying to Epstien 'Do you want this film to be made?'

Epstien was saying 'Under no circumstances will this film ever be made.'

Lilia thought — So that's all right.

Lisa Grant said 'Then what's the point of our trip?'

Wolf Tanner said 'What's the point of any of our trips?'

The hostess was standing by Lilia and saying 'I've got your things.' She was holding Lilia's zip-bag, the child's push-chair, and the man's almost-empty bottle of whisky.

Lilia thought — Now I will start crying again.

She said 'Oh you are terribly kind!'

Jane was saying 'But does anyone know what happened at Lod airport?'

Spud was saying 'Yes, two men were shot on the runway. There was a diversion.'

Jason was thinking — There are those things going on elsewhere —

Lilia was thinking — But what else could have happened if he wanted to hurt my child?

Jason said 'We're coming down now.'

His child said 'My don't want to come down!'

Jason said 'But we're coming down by the sea! There will be sand, and fishes!'

Lilia said 'Would you like some of his whisky?'

176

Jason thought — What a way to get whisky!

Lilia said 'I feel so sad.'

Jason had taken his script from Lilia and was putting it into his bag.

He thought — That bird, flying around, would it never have come down?

XXII

SCENE: a villa on the bay of Naples, 79 A.D. A terrace over-
looking the sea.

Vesuvius is in the background. It glows brightly. The sky
above it from time to time changes colour.

Josephus, dressed in Roman clothes, walks up and down.
He moves with a limp.

Berenice is reclining on a garden seat.

It is as if Josephus were rehearsing a speech —

    JOSEPHUS

  — To be an outcast from all nations!

  A serpent! Cain! Not to be part of any society! —

He breaks off to look out over the balustrade at Vesuvius.

    JOSEPHUS

I say, those buggers are getting it at Pompeii!

    BERENICE

Who's it for?

    JOSEPHUS

The bonfire?

My speech?

The Capri Antiquities Religious and Dramatic Society.
CARDS for short.

He glances into the camera.

    BERENICE

Are you often invited?

    JOSEPHUS

Last month I gave a paper on — Sodom, the Myth and
the Agony.

He looks out over the balustrade.

Then he beats his chest and acts —

    JOSEPHUS

  — My fault! My fault! My own most grievous fault! —

BERENICE
What did you say?

JOSEPHUS
I said — If you start off gently enough, then, when you seem to be on fire —

BERENICE
No, I mean, to the Roman general.

JOSEPHUS
Oh.

He walks up and down.

JOSEPHUS
Well, I was taken to him in chains. I drew myself up. I said — One day you will be Emperor!

BERENICE
And he was —

JOSEPHUS
Yes.

Well, someone had to be.

What you say, you influence.

It's called —

BERENICE
I don't care what it's called!

JOSEPHUS
The Anthropic Cosmological Principle.

What a dreadful phrase!

He grimaces, and holds his leg as if in pain.

BERENICE
Were you really hurt?

JOSEPHUS
What do you mean, was I really hurt!

BERENICE
One never knows with you.

JOSEPHUS
They don't like it if you're happy. I was in chains.

He watches Vesuvius. The sky darkens.

After a time —

JOSEPHUS
Why do birds of paradise have long tails?

179

BERENICE

I don't know, why do birds of paradise have long tails?

JOSEPHUS

They learn to survive, because they see life's difficult.

He walks up and down.

BERENICE

Is that true?

JOSEPHUS

Well, they don't really know yet.

It's like the giraffe syndrome.

He glances into the camera.

BERENICE

What is the giraffe syndrome?

JOSEPHUS

People think giraffes have long necks because they stretch up to the tops of trees. But in fact, they just happen to have long necks, and then one day, bang! there are only leaves at the tops of trees —

BERENICE

So they survive —

JOSEPHUS

Yes —

BERENICE

And it's like that with you.

JOSEPHUS

Oh one never knows with me!

He watches Vesuvius. The sky becomes red.

BERENICE

And Philomela?

JOSEPHUS

What about Philomela —

BERENICE

How did she survive?

Josephus walks up and down again with his limp.

JOSEPHUS

— I say, my good man, will you take me to your leader —

BERENICE

And they did?

JOSEPHUS
— I have a message —
BERENICE
What —
JOSEPHUS
— These children are immortal —
BERENICE
And they believed that?
JOSEPHUS
Oh, they'll believe —
— The children that survive are the children that survive.
It's a tautology.
BERENICE
What isn't —
JOSEPHUS
What has three legs in the morning, three legs in the afternoon, and three legs in the evening —
He crouches and slaps his thigh, and does a little dance as if he were a comic.
Then he seems to remember he should have a limp.
BERENICE
She went to bed with him?
JOSEPHUS
Who?
BERENICE
Her Roman general.
Josephus frowns.
JOSEPHUS
Oh yes I think one has to, you know.
Then one or two can leave the theatre.
He glances into the camera.
BERENICE
She's lucky —
JOSEPHUS
Who?
BERENICE
Philomela.

JOSEPHUS

Sh!

He puts a hand to his lips.

He looks out at the side of the terrace, left, as if there might be someone listening. Then he acts —

JOSEPHUS

— I'm too old! I try, but I can't satisfy her! —

Then he comes and puts a hand on Berenice's head.

He says quietly —

JOSEPHUS

You could stay here.

BERENICE

How —

He walks up and down again. He acts —

JOSEPHUS

— By sitting in a bowl of rose-leaves and drawing fire up through your arse: then its exploding in your head like a volcano —

He watches Vesuvius.

After a time —

BERENICE

What are you writing now?

JOSEPHUS

A long and boring work. On the antiquities of the Jews.

BERENICE

I'm one of the antiquities of the Jews.

JOSEPHUS

You've got a long neck.

He comes and looks down on her. Then he kisses her.

Philomela comes in. She is carrying a tray with drinks. She puts the tray on a table.

Then she goes to the balustrade and looks over.

PHILOMELA

I say, those buggers are getting it at Pompeii!

Josephus seems to listen. Then he says loudly —

JOSEPHUS

— What I'm saying in my book, my lecture, is that the Jews are, or could be, the giraffes with long necks. Of course, I have to do an enormous amount of research into this —

PHILOMELA

Yes I do go to bed with the Emperor —

Josephus says even more loudly —

JOSEPHUS

The interesting thing is, there always are leaves at the tops of trees —

BERENICE

— He's always on a horse. It affects his legs. So they built a triumphal arch to him —

Josephus looks down at her.

JOSEPHUS

Yes, that sort of thing: witty —

PHILOMELA

It's a very scholarly book. No one will understand it.

JOSEPHUS

Tell that to the Capri Antiquities Religious and Dramatic Society —

That'll kill them.

He goes to the side of the terrace on the left and seems to listen to try to find out if anyone has been listening. After a time —

PHILOMELA

It's all right, everyone's gone to watch the fireworks.

Philomela gives Berenice a drink.

PHILOMELA

They put bits of offal on our doorstep.

BERENICE

They send packets of shit to me.

Josephus walks up and down. He acts —

JOSEPHUS

— Oh what shall we do! —

PHILOMELA

Put it on the cabbages.

Josephus comes and stands by Philomela. They hold hands. They look down at Berenice.

JOSEPHUS

You could be dead, underneath the volcano.

Berenice puts her head in her hands.

Josephus lays his head on Philomela's shoulder.

JOSEPHUS

I tried to start a legend about how there were seven just Jews in any generation who kept the world going —

PHILOMELA

Seven?

JOSEPHUS

And the writer —

And the writer's muse!

He looks down on Berenice.

There is a shower of sparks from Vesuvius.

Berenice takes her head from her hands. She seems to have been crying.

BERENICE

What are we then?

JOSEPHUS

The towers we build of ourselves.

BERENICE

And what are gods?

PHILOMELA

Birds that fly around for ever.

Lava pours down from Vesuvius.

The Old Woman, from Jotapata and Masada, comes in carrying a tray of food. She puts it down on the table.

OLD WOMAN

They say the old Emperor has come alive again and is living with his woman beyond Pompeii.

JOSEPHUS

You can't say that!

He puts his head in his hands.

OLD WOMAN

They say that some gods came down in an egg the other day, and are waiting to hatch out by the Red Sea.

She sets out the food and the drink. Then she waits for the others to come to the table.

OLD WOMAN

There was a man tried to fly in Rome the other day —

BERENICE

What happened?

PHILOMELA

He went into a tree.

They settle round the table, to drink and eat.

BERENICE

What will we be like?

JOSEPHUS

Two arms, two heads, and one in between.

BERENICE

And the children?

OLD WOMAN

What of the children —

BERENICE

What are you teaching them?

PHILOMELA

The serpent was the angel who woke Adam and Eve
from their sleep in the garden —

OLD WOMAN

And the mark on the forehead of Cain is the eye that
survives because it sees inwards —

JOSEPHUS

You can't say that!

OLD WOMAN

I didn't say that!
They have to find it.

PHILOMELA

Here they are!

She glances into the camera, as if at the audience.
Berenice looks at the camera; she speaks as if to the
audience.

BERENICE

Were you tortured?

JOSEPHUS

You'll survive.

XXIII

On a green and gold beach with mountains a pale grey above it
as if clouds had come down to cover the land and procreate a
new form of life there —

Jason and Lilia lay on the beach and watched their child
playing by the edge of the water.

The only other people on the beach were a young Israeli
couple who had appeared walking hand in hand and who now
seemed to be looking for something in the sea. The man was
tall and bearded and wore army uniform; the girl wore a shirt
and shorts and had strong brown legs. Jason thought — She is
like Judith; without the head of Holofernes. Then — I must
make contact with Judith when I get home.

Lilia said 'But don't you mind if truth isn't knowing exactly
what happened, on the plane?'

Jason said 'Oh you make things up as you go along anyway.'

The couple were bending down and peering into the water.
Jason thought — Or like that young couple who might have
mislaid their child on their way to Egypt.

Lilia said 'But about the past — '

Jason said 'Well, what you see is just what's left anyway.'

Their child seemed to have picked up something out of the
water. He was holding it and watching the young couple.

Lilia said 'But there's a real war going on.'

Jason said 'Yes, they can kill you.'

Lilia said 'You do think it's more than luck if you stay alive?'

Jason said 'That's what you can't talk about.'

The young couple on the beach had taken off some of their
clothes and were lying down. They seemed to be about to
make love.

Jason said 'I mean, it's to do with your mind, but your mind's
not built to keep hold of it.'

He thought — That girl who is like Judith has her shorts slit open at the thigh and from that cave which is like the head of Holofernes there are birds now flying —

Lilia said 'You can work for it?'

Jason said ' — Make an art-work of it?'

Lilia thought — The words for love are so banal!

Their child, watching the young couple by the sea, held from his hand something that swung like a pendulum.

Lilia said 'Aren't children supposed to think that people are killing each other when they make love?'

Jason said 'You think that couple will get a trauma?'

He thought — The words have changed: there are circuits; subject verb subject. It is we who are frightened if children watch us making love.

Lilia said 'Shall I call him?'

Jason said 'No.'

He thought — Not in this landscape, womb, where promised life began: where people searched amongst hills and deserts as if between breasts and thighs —

Lilia thought — That young couple are like things that have crawled up from the sea or are resting on their journey into Egypt —

— It is as if our child were their child? Its father?

She said 'You know that place where we are walking through a wood — '

Jason said 'What?' Then — 'Oh yes — '

Lilia said 'And then suddenly you write it as if we were people in our own story — '

Jason thought — The things you remember! this network! meetings by the sea —

She said 'Why did you write it like that?'

He said 'There's an old Jewish myth that when God created the world the words that would describe it were themselves being created. This was what creation was: something together with its language. What distinguished it from chaos.'

She said 'And that's what we know — '

He thought — Words? Creation? Love?

He said 'People are myth-makers. But what happens, what's

known, when one knows one makes myths?'

Lilia thought — Really, that young couple and the child: they are more like a picture of Adam and Eve in the Garden, and the serpent is watching them.

She said 'Well, what is known?'

He said 'One is not frightened any more.'

She said 'And that's all?'

He said 'All!'

Lilia thought — One is watching the child, who is like the serpent, who is watching the couple making love.

She said 'Like God.'

He said 'Yes like God.'

She said 'And the rest is boring.'

He said 'And the rest is boring.'

She said 'And lives or dies.'

The child had gone up to the young couple and was talking to them on the beach.

Lilia said 'But which?'

He said 'If you know there's a which — '

He thought — Which: witch: these words, connections, are like love: they make things live.

Lilia said 'What do you think he's saying to them?'

Jason said 'I expect he's telling them about what happened when he was borned.'

She said 'And what do you think they're saying to him?'

He said 'Perhaps they're telling him about making love.'

Lilia thought — There is a vision, dream, in some book, isn't there, of beautiful people walking on a beach: and what makes them beautiful is a temple where witches are dismembering a child —

Jason said 'It's like *The Magic Mountain*.'

Lilia said 'Yes, *The Magic Mountain*!'

She thought — But the child is all right!

Jason said 'I think I should get those children to appear round the tea-table: the ones that have survived.'

Lilia thought — Oh yes. Then — I thought we were the children —

She said 'You're still making it up as you go along?'

188

He said 'Yes it's still making itself up as I go along.'

Lilia thought — It's all we've ever been together, known together, and then what happens, that survives —

Their child was running towards them across the sand. He said 'Mummy — '

She said 'Yes?'

Her child said 'Look what those people have gived to me!'

He was holding one end of a chain on the other end of which was a medallion. Lilia thought — It spins too fast: the images are indecipherable.

An armoured car had appeared at the end of the beach. It sat there like some crab.

Lilia said 'How extraordinarily kind!'

The child said 'My find it in the sea!'

Lilia thought — But how could they have given it to you if you found it in the sea?

Her child said 'My could!'

At the top of the armoured car a man's head had appeared: then his naked body.

Jason thought — The man is like a baby turtle about to run down towards the sea.

The couple on the beach had sat up and were watching Lilia and Jason.

Lilia thought — It is when too many images come in at once that lights come on as if in a theatre —

The naked man jumped out of the armoured car and ran down towards the sea.

Lilia said 'They're very beautiful.'

Jason said 'Who?'

He thought — The crab is sending the baby turtles out, not catching them —

— What is that myth about particles of light that have been trapped in matter?

Lilia said 'Do you think we should give it back?'

Jason said 'No.'

The child said 'It's mine!'

Jason took hold of the medallion. On one side was embossed the image of a snake with its tail in its mouth: on the other, the image of a bird carrying in its beak what looked like a flower.

Jason gave the medallion back to the child. The child ran towards the couple on the beach.

Lilia said 'We mustn't put too much on to him.'

Out of the top of the armoured car another man's head had appeared. Jason was thinking — But if what is being liberated is light, will millions emerge like dandelion seeds —

— She loves me: she loves me not —

The second man, naked, ran down to swim in the sea.

Lilia said 'Perhaps there's peace.'

Jason thought — Or even if there's war, from such soft dragons' teeth —

The young couple had got up and were coming towards them. They held the child by the hand.

Jason thought — She loves me —

Then — I mean, new life will grow.

The young man said 'Hullo.'

Lilia said 'Hullo.'

Jason was thinking — Yes, indeed, she is like that frightening Indian goddess Kali: turn her over and you get the beautiful goddess Devi —

The girl said 'Hullo.'

Jason said 'Hullo.'

The young man said 'We wanted to give your child that medallion, which he found in the sea.'

The girl said 'It was ours, but we'd lost it.'

The young man said 'We've got another one just like it.'

Lilia said 'That's terribly kind!'

She thought — Of course, my child was right.

She took the medallion and turned it this way and that.

Jason said 'Do you know if the snake eating itself is a symbol of life?'

The young man said 'Oh yes, I think so.'

The girl said 'It is making love to itself.'

The young man said 'It is being born.'

The girl said 'Your child was telling us about how everything in fact is all right inside you when you are born.'

The young man said 'He is an extraordinary child.'

Jason, reaching for the medallion, thought — How could one talk about this meeting? Such things are still taboo.

Lilia was thinking — We are like people who have landed on some strange planet —

The young man said 'It's from Masada.'

Jason said 'Masada!'

The girl said 'The medallion.'

Jason took it from Lilia and turned it this way and that.

He thought — We are those people from the cave who have been liberated like light —

His child said 'Mummy — '

Lilia said 'Yes?'

The child said 'These people were making love.'

The young man put his arm round the waist of the girl and laughed.

The girl said 'He said — What are you hiding?'

Lilia said 'Hiding!'

The young man said 'Ah, perhaps we will now have a child!'

A third man, naked, had got out of the top of the armoured car and was running down towards the sea.

Lilia thought — We were walking through the wood and it was ourselves that we saw walking —

Jason thought — What is the world outside the cave: in this strange sun?

The girl said 'My name is Deborah Kahn and this is my husband David.'

Lilia said 'My name is Lilia and this is my husband Jason.'

Jason said 'How do you do.'

Deborah said 'How do you do.'

David said 'You are interested in myths?'

Jason said 'Yes.' Then — 'You mean, you found this at Masada?'

David said 'Yes, I found them in a cave near the southern bastion, when I was climbing on the rock-face. There is some evidence that the cave was once used by Gnostics.'

Jason said 'I didn't know there were Gnostics on Masada.'

David said 'Or rather, perhaps it was where the people who survived the suicide pact were hiding.'

There was the noise of distant gunfire: or of thunder, behind hills.

Lilia said 'But it's precious!'

Deborah said to the child 'Yes, you must keep it secret. Or people might take it from you.'

Lilia said 'But it's too good of you — '

Deborah said 'No.'

The child held out his hand.

David said 'Look!' He took the medallion from Jason.

Then he made a gesture as if throwing the medallion into the air. He opened his mouth and then seemed to swallow.

The child said 'But that's not the trick!'

David held his hand to his stomach and seemed to produce the medallion from it. Then he held this out to the child.

The child took it. He said 'And where's the other one?'

Deborah said 'Ah, you are really clever!'

David Kahn opened his other hand and there was another medallion in it. He said 'So you needn't even do a trick!'

Deborah Kahn said 'We each can have one all the time.'

Lilia said 'That's the secret?'

The child laughed.

Jason looked round at the green and gold landscape: the mountains as if clouds had come down.

He said 'Isn't this near where Moses spoke to God?'

David said 'Moses only saw God's arse.'

Deborah said 'But you couldn't say you'd seen God's face, could you?'

NICHOLAS MOSLEY

Hopeful Monsters

'Quite simply, the best English novel to have been written since the Second World War'
A. N. Wilson, *Evening Standard*

'This is a major novel by any standard of measurement. Its ambition is lofty, its intelligence startling, and its sympathy profound. It is frequently funny, sometimes painful, sometimes moving. It asks fundamental questions about the nature of experience . . . It is a novel which makes the greater part of contemporary fiction seem pygmy in comparison'

Allan Massie, *The Scotsman*

'A gigantic achievement that glows and grows long after it is put aside'
Jennifer Potter, *Independent on Sunday*

'Enormously ambitious and continuously fascinating . . . There is an intellectual engagement here, a devouring determination to investigate, to refrain from judgement while never abandoning moral conventions, that is rare among British novelists – for that matter, among novelists of any nationality'
Paul Binding, *New Statesman and Society*

'Nicholas Mosley, in a country never generous to experimental writing, is one of the more significant instances we have that it can still, brilliantly, be done'
Malcolm Bradbury

CHRISTOPHER ISHERWOOD

A Single Man

'George, the middle-fiftyish English don at the Californian
university, has lost his boyfriend, killed in a motor crash.
He carries on with his life, making faces at the children in
the nearby houses, lecturing on Aldous Huxley, gossiping
with other members of the teaching staff, drinking too
much with a fellow expatriate who has been abandoned
by her husband. All the time he is tormented by his urges:
the sight of a blond young man playing tennis, a chance
meeting with one of his students for whom George has
been nursing a passion which leads to drunken nude
bathing. Mr Isherwood has not written anything as good
as this for a long time. It is all very sad and yet at times
wildly funny . . . The description of the Californian scene
is bitter, nostalgic, yet at the same time tinged with love'
David Holloway, Daily Telegraph

'In *A Single Man*, published in the mid-sixties, [Isher-
wood] produced what seems now the most accurate and
far-sighted of all the novels written in and about that
difficult decade'
Books and Bookmen

'A testimony to Isherwood's undiminished brilliance as a
novelist'
Anthony Burgess, The Listener

CHRISTOPHER ISHERWOOD

Goodbye to Berlin

The narrator of *Goodbye to Berlin* is called "Christopher Isherwood" ("Herr Issyvoo"). His story, in this novel, first published in 1939, obliquely evokes the gathering storm in Berlin before and just after the rise to power of the Nazis. Events are seen through the eyes of a series of individuals: his landlady, Fraülein Schroeder; Sally Bowles, the English upper-class waif; the Nowaks, a struggling working-class family; the Landauers, a wealthy, civilized family of Jewish store owners, whose lives are about to be ruined.

Wry, detached, impressionistic in its approach, yet vividly eloquent about the brutal effect of public events on private lives, *Goodbye to Berlin* has provided the inspiration for a highly successful stage play, *I Am a Camera*, and the stage and screen musical, *Cabaret*. It has long been recognized as one of the most powerful and popular novels written in English in this century.

'Mr Isherwood is revealed as a genuine humorist. The book as a whole throws a vivid light on the historical background of Hitler's rise to power'
Yorkshire Post

'How to render in fiction what seemed more grotesquely fictional than anything that could be imagined? Isherwood . . . took the oblique view, suggesting by his own brand of resonant understatement the full extent of the political emptiness and personal despair that lay beneath the brittle surface'
Books and Bookmen

GILBERT ADAIR

Love and Death on Long Island

'A latter-day and very English reworking of the *Death in Venice* theme . . . it is a little gem of a book, beautifully written and constructed, superbly characterised. What disturbs is the sheer elegance of Adair's prose style — most of us had probably forgotten that English could be written so well . . . A *tour de force*'
Anne Smith, Literary Review

'[It] is in a direct line from *Lolita* and (as the title implies) *Death in Venice* and comparisons with Nabokov or Mann are not out of place. Brief, pure, intense, and as almost ludicrously desperate as all tales of impossible love must be . . . with perfect poise and poignance, in a shimmering, cold prose, Adair puts across the impossibility of fulfilment, the heat and humiliations of passion. The writing is masterly, the conjuring of contrasting worlds a triumph'
Isabel Quigly, Financial Times

'Quibbles vanish beside the force of his slyly erotic and erudite prose in this beautifully executed literary pastiche'
Independent on Sunday

'A concoction which is as memorable as a night in the stalls of the human psyche ought to be'
Tom Adair, Scotland on Sunday

EVA FIGES

The Tree of Knowledge

'In fact, Milton's daughter was discovered in poverty and then kept by the charity of the curious. Her grandfather was ruined in the Civil War. He never paid John Milton for his daughter's dowry, and she was persecuted for the want of it. A woman without property had no prospects, except marrying an old man with desires no lower than his stomach. With a humane comprehension of right speech, Eva Figes makes Milton's daughter breathe again, and deliver a homily against male oppression, which her father would never have admitted, for all his talk of freedom for men and the right for divorce. This is the apple of wisdom that the serpent of experience has given to this new Eve, who cannot regain the paradise that men like her father have lost for her'

Andrew Sinclair, The Times

'This is a woman's version of literary history, a deeply felt response to the smug argument that "genius" is something to be pampered and cosseted . . . As a commentary on the domestic and intellectual deprivations suffered by women during (and not only during) this period, *The Tree of Knowledge* is totally compelling: but its ambitions go further than that. It is not simply about "knowledge" in the sense of learning because, as the final chapter makes movingly clear, Deborah Milton has been denied not only her education but the very right to give voice to her knowledge of herself'

Jonathan Coe, Guardian

NICHOLAS MOSLEY

Imago Bird

'An inventive, wickedly amusing coming-of-age novel . . .
Mosley shapes a narrative the way a nuclear physicist
might track a quantum experiment in thousands of dis-
crete moments, recording his characters' immediate
sense impressions, the gap between what they speak and
what is churning within'
Publishers Weekly

'Nicholas Mosley gets all of it – psychoanalysis, youthful
sex, and politics – exactly and hilariously right. He is
ingenious and cunning . . . Anybody who is serious about
the state of English fiction should applaud Mosley's au-
dacity – his skill is unquestionable'
Frank Rudman, *Spectator*

'*Imago Bird* is a convincing account of a highly intelligent adolescent confronted by a random and discon-
tinuous world'
Peter Ackroyd, *Sunday Times*

'There is a sharp, elliptical quality about Nicholas
Mosley's writing that constantly checks the flow of words
and prevents you letting the story engulf you. The plot of
Imago Bird is simple enough: it's the angular telling that
gives its piercing, metallic quality'
Martyn Goff, *Daily Telegraph*

'Mosley has a genuinely original view of the world,
making *Imago Bird* the most interesting novel I have
read for some time'
Thomas Hinde, *Sunday Telegraph*

CHRISTOPHER ISHERWOOD

Prater Violet

Set in London in the mid-1930s *Prater Violet* explores
the relationship between Viennese film director
Friedrich Bergmann, brought to London by Imperial
Bulldog Pictures to direct a film, and Christopher Isherwood, hired to write the script. Against the background
of the plight of Austria and the rise of fascism, the novel
counterpoints the true role and limits of the artist with
the fatuous nature of the film Bergmann is directing, a
sickly and sentimental period romance.

At once a comic portrait of the film industry and a
serious analysis of the relationship between art and life,
this book marked a turning point in Isherwood's writing
– the first to be written after his spiritual conversion. But
above all it endures as one of the most accomplished
short novels of the century – a sophisticated, witty book
with a subtle and questing inner depth.

'The best prose writer in English'
Gore Vidal

CHRISTOPHER ISHERWOOD

All the Conspirators

Isherwood's theme, in a novel which clearly shows his early influences, was to recur in his later work: the destruction of the son by the evil mother. In the Kensington of the 1920s — silver frames, inlaid bureaux, charming sitting-rooms — the "conspirators", Philip and Joan, fight to throw off the oppressive power of their mother.

In Isherwood's own words, *All The Conspirators* is the story of "a trivial but furious battle which the combatants fight out passionately and dirtily to the finish, using whatever weapons come to their hands."

'This first novel is a key to Isherwood and the twenties. It is as mature, as readable, as concentrated as anything he has written since'
Cyril Connolly

'The best prose writer in English'
Gore Vidal

A Selected List of Titles Available from Minerva

While every effort is made to keep prices low, it is sometimes necessary to increase prices at short notice. Mandarin Paperbacks reserves the right to show new retail prices on covers which may differ from those previously advertised in the text or elsewhere.

The prices shown below were correct at the time of going to press.

Fiction

☐	7493 9026 3	**I Pass Like Night**	Jonathan Ames	£3.99	BX
☐	7493 9006 9	**The Tidewater Tales**	John Bath	£4.99	BX
☐	7493 9004 2	**A Casual Brutality**	Neil Blessondath	£4.50	BX
☐	7493 9028 2	**Interior**	Justin Cartwright	£3.99	BC
☐	7493 9002 6	**No Telephone to Heaven**	Michelle Cliff	£3.99	BX
☐	7493 9028 X	**Not Not While the Giro**	James Kelman	£4.50	BX
☐	7493 9011 5	**Parable of the Blind**	Gert Hofmann	£3.99	BC
☐	7493 9010 7	**The Inventor**	Jakov Lind	£3.99	BC
☐	7493 9003 4	**Fall of the Imam**	Nawal El Saadewi	£3.99	BC

Non-Fiction

☐	7493 9012 3	**Days in the Life**	Jonathon Green	£4.99	BC
☐	7493 9019 0	**In Search of J D Salinger**	Ian Hamilton	£4.99	BX
☐	7493 9023 9	**Stealing from a Deep Place**	Brian Hall	£3.99	BX
☐	7493 9005 0	**The Orton Diaries**	John Lahr	£5.99	BC
☐	7493 9014 X	**Nora**	Brenda Maddox	£6.99	BC

All these books are available at your bookshop or newsagent, or can be ordered direct from the publisher. Just tick the titles you want and fill in the form below. Available in:
BX: British Commonwealth excluding Canada
BC: British Commonwealth including Canada

Mandarin Paperbacks, Cash Sales Department, PO Box 11, Falmouth, Cornwall TR10 9EN.

Please send cheque or postal order, no currency, for purchase price quoted and allow the following for postage and packing:

UK	80p for the first book, 20p for each additional book ordered to a maximum charge of £2.00.
BFPO	80p for the first book, 20p for each additional book.
Overseas including Eire	£1.50 for the first book, £1.00 for the second and 30p for each additional book thereafter.

NAME (Block letters) ....

ADDRESS ....

....

....